The Bar Tab Also Rises

A Lost Generation Comedy

The Bar Tab Also Rises

A Lost Generation Comedy

By Brian Burns

REVELATION 1:8 PUBLISHERS

REVELATION 1:8 PUBLISHERS

ISBN: 979-8-9997192-1-8

About This Book

The Bar Tab Also Rises is a comedy parody inspired by Ernest Hemingway's classic novel *The Sun Also Rises*, which is now in the public domain.

While Hemingway's original explored the "Lost Generation" of Americans living in post-World War I Paris and Spain, this version reimagines those same characters as spectacularly self-absorbed expatriates whose biggest problems involve interpretive dance emergencies, cartoon rat obsessions, supernatural poultry attacks, and a mysterious curse.

Instead of attending traditional bullfights in Pamplona, they witness the far more dangerous "Running of the Roosters." Meanwhile, everyone drinks enough alcohol to float a small yacht while complaining about their impossibly privileged lives and debating whether theme parks that don't exist are worth visiting.

From the gothic cafés of Paris to the fish-themed amusement parks of rural Spain, this story escalates from merely absurd to completely unhinged.

Readers familiar with the original will recognize the structure and themes transformed through a lens of modern absurdity, while newcomers can simply enjoy the chaotic adventures of Americans living abroad who have too much money, too much time, and far too little perspective on their own lives.

CONTENTS

Book I: The Tab Opens

Chapter 1: Robert Cohn the Dance Champion

Robert Cohn was once interpretive dance champion of Princeton. Now, I know what you're thinking: "Wow, Princeton interpretive dance champion, that's like being the most articulate mime at a silent film festival." But it meant everything to Cohn. The man treated this accomplishment like he'd discovered the secret to human expression, when really he'd just learned to flail around dramatically while other trust fund babies sat in an auditorium pretending to understand his "emotional journey."

He didn't even like interpretive dance at first. This is like becoming a professional librarian because you hate books. But Cohn learned to dance because—and I'm not making this up—people were mean to him for his habit of critiquing everyone else's complete 'lack of authenticity' and for spreading expensive condiments on everything he ate, including dessert, at Princeton. One such condiment was Beige Poupon—it was nothing more than expensive mustard. One bottle cost as much as someone's monthly wage and Cohn made sure everyone knew he was using it.

His instructor, Madame Cordelia (and yes, she insisted on being called "Madame," despite being from New Jersey), taught all her students to dance like they were channeling the spirits of dying swans. This was Cordelia's brilliant philosophy: make everyone move like they're having an emotional breakdown, regardless of whether they were expressing "the agony of unrequited love" or "the joy of a spring morning."

But here's the kicker: Madame Cordelia immediately entered Cohn into competitions he had no business being in, and he got his nose permanently flattened during a particularly ambitious interpretive piece about "the futility of modern existence." Apparently, he collided with another dancer during what was supposed to be a graceful representation of "souls passing in the night." Cohn learned to dance to feel better about himself, then immediately got his face rearranged while expressing his feelings about loneliness. It's like writing a poem about all your childhood trauma that is immediately mocked. But somehow, this made Cohn feel better about interpretive dance. The man's got the logic of a pretzel doing yoga.

Now, I have to admit something: I don't trust anyone who dances. Especially when they're telling me about their glory days while we're sitting in a Parisian café at 2 PM on a Tuesday, somehow affording wine that costs more than most people's rent. So, I went and checked with Madame herself. And wouldn't you know it? The story was true. Madame not only remembered Cohn, but she'd also been wondering what happened to him. Probably because Cohn still owed her money.

Here's where it gets really rich: Robert Cohn came from not one, but two kinds of wealthy families in New York. Through his father's side, he was new money rich. Through his mother's side, he was old money rich. This man hit the genetic lottery twice and still managed to develop an inferiority complex. It's like complaining about having too many swimming pools.

At military school (because of course he went to military school), nobody cared about his pretentious critiques. He played football, made friends, and probably had his laundry done by servants—the works. But the minute he got to Princeton, suddenly everyone's a critic. And instead of just ignoring these people Cohn decided, "Clearly, I need to express myself with dance."

So, he danced his way through Princeton, graduated with a flattened nose and enough emotional baggage to fill a freight train, and immediately married the first woman who was nice to him. Because nothing says "healthy relationship foundation" like "she didn't immediately insult my personality."

Five years of marriage, three kids, and boom—he's blown through most of his fifty-thousand-dollar inheritance. Fifty thousand! In 1920s money! That's like spending a million dollars on… I don't know, what do rich people waste money on? Probably gold-plated tennis rackets and caviar for their pets. Also, it turns out the "Cohn Dance Studio of Pretentious Emotions" wasn't such a great use of the money.

Here's the other thing that kills me: during all this time, Cohn's mother had set him up with an allowance of three hundred dollars a month. Three hundred 1920s dollars! That's like getting a monthly check for several thousand dollars today, just for existing. And we're supposed to feel sorry for this guy?

But wait, I should give credit where it's due—the man is a gifted narcissist. Case in point: All of a sudden, Cohn decided he wanted to leave his wife. In his warped mind, she was obviously stifling his artistic genius—because clearly the problem couldn't be that he wasn't any good at interpretive dance. No, it had to be someone else's fault. So just when Cohn finally works up the courage to leave his wife—and I'm talking months of inner monologue here, like Hamlet but with more whining—*she leaves him!* For a miniature painter. Not even a regular-sized painter! A miniature painter! The ultimate insult: getting dumped for someone whose entire profession involves making tiny pictures.

The best part? Cohn had convinced himself that leaving would be "too cruel" because his wife couldn't possibly survive without him. Meanwhile, she's already packed her bags and moved in with someone who paints dollhouse portraits for a living.

So, what does our hero do? He moves to Broadway and immediately falls in with "Show People." You know, the kind of folks who use "summer" as a verb and discuss the "authenticity" of their suffering while sipping champagne. Since Cohn still had some of daddy's money left, he naturally became the financial backer of a Broadway show. Because nothing screams "I'm a serious artist" like buying your way in.

The show was nothing more than a two-hour solo interpretive dance by Cohn himself. If that's not bad enough he thought dressing in a clown costume would add to the emotional effect. By the time it closed (because of course it closed), Cohn had gone from silent investor to sole producer. He discovered he liked having authority, although he was also his only employee.

But here's where our story gets really interesting. A woman—let's call her Frances, because that was her name—

decided that Cohn and his show were her tickets to the big time. She "took him in hand," which is a polite way of saying she managed his life like he was an expensive pet. And she had an expensive pet, a Pomeranian she called Poopsy-Pops, which she made Cohn take care of. And Cohn, being Cohn, was absolutely certain he loved her.

When Frances realized the show wasn't going to make her famous, she did what any reasonable person would do: she convinced Cohn to move to Europe so he could "dance." Because apparently, the only way to become a real dancer is to drink wine in Paris while complaining about Americans. It's like a law or something.

They spent three years in Europe—one year traveling (because why settle down when you can afford to wander aimlessly?) and two years in Paris. During this entire time, Cohn had exactly two friends: Braddocks and me. Braddocks was his "dance friend" (translation: they discussed dance while drinking), and I was his "tennis friend" (translation: we hit balls around while drinking).

Meanwhile, Frances started noticing that she was getting older, and her attitude toward Cohn shifted from casual exploitation to desperate marriage plotting. Because nothing says "romantic commitment" like panicking about your expiring looks.

For two and a half years, I swear, Cohn didn't look at another woman; with all that dancing no other woman was really looking at him either. He spent his time being "fairly happy" (which in Cohn-speak means "mildly dissatisfied but too polite to complain"), except for the fact that he'd rather be in America. You know, because living in Paris on an allowance while pursuing your artistic dreams is apparently such a hardship.

I got a glimpse into Frances's warped mind one night after dinner. We'd eaten at Le Overpriced then went to Café de Pretentious for coffee and several rounds of after-dinner drinks. Because apparently, our biggest problem in life was not having enough places to drink.

Cohn had shown up wearing his cream-colored cable-knit sweater (the one with the little anchor pattern) and carrying a small jar of Beige Poupon, which he'd insisted on spreading on everything despite the waiter's horrified expression. He was also carrying Poopsy-Pops, Frances's ridiculous Pomeranian, in a tiny Louis Vuitton carrier. The dog was wearing a miniature beret that matched Frances's outfit.

"Robert, darling, Poopsy-Pops needs her evening constitutional," Frances had announced during dessert, which meant Cohn had to excuse himself to walk a five-pound furball around the block while we finished our cognac.

When he returned, Cohn started talking about taking a weekend trip—just the two of us guys, you understand. He wanted to get out of town and go fishing. I was shocked, Cohn actually wanting to do something normal? Though knowing him, he'd probably pack his Princeton interpretive dance varsity jacket and try to express the essence of trout through movement.

I suggested we go to Strasbourg and mentioned I knew a girl there who could show us around. That's when Frances kicked me under the table. Hard. Poopsy-Pops let out a tiny yip of alarm from her lap.

I thought it was an accident and kept talking about this perfectly nice American girl who'd been living in Strasbourg for two years. Another kick. This time I looked up and saw Frances's face transforming into something that belonged in a horror movie. Even Poopsy-Pops seemed to sense the danger and burrowed deeper into her tiny cashmere blanket.

"I mean who likes girls?" I said, quickly backtracking, "why go to Strasbourg? We could go to Chippendales or something."

Suddenly, Cohn looked relieved, and the kicking stopped. Frances began cooing to Poopsy-Pops again, and the little dog poked her head out cautiously.

Amazing how quickly the temperature can change when you accidentally threaten someone's romantic monopoly.

After I said goodnight and left, Cohn followed me out, claiming he needed to buy a paper. He was still carrying the dog in the carrier and had somehow managed to get Beige Poupon on his sweater sleeve.

"Why did you mention that girl in Strasbourg?" he asked. "Didn't you see Frances?"

"Well, I didn't know she was a complete psychopath. You better watch out with that one."

"It doesn't make any difference. If any girl is there I couldn't go." He shifted the dog carrier to his other arm as Poopsy-Pops whimpered softly.

Any girl? Not even a specific girl he was interested in? Just the theoretical possibility of female companionship was enough to send Frances into full territorial mode.

"You don't know Frances," Cohn said. "Any girl at all. Didn't you see the way she looked?" He glanced nervously back toward the café, where Frances was probably already planning his punishment for this conversation.

So, we settled on Senlis instead. A nice, safe, presumably girl-free destination where two grown men could take walks in the woods and pretend this was somehow meaningful. Though I had a feeling Cohn would end up carrying dog treats and a portable water bowl for Poopsy-Pops instead of fishing gear.

As I watched Cohn walk back to the café with his paper, still juggling the dog carrier and trying to wipe Beige Poupon off his sweater, I couldn't help but think: this poor guy has gone from Princeton interpretive dance champion to trust fund dance studio owner to a kept man in Paris who's basically a full-time dog nanny, and somehow he's convinced himself this is all perfectly normal. Little did I know that winter would bring changes that would make his current level of annoying seem quaint by comparison.

But then again, who am I to judge? I'm sitting in cafés at midnight, drinking expensive liquor, writing about it, and calling it literature.

Chapter 2: Cohn Discovers Ratty Rat

In the winter of 1924, Robert Cohn went over to America with his interpretive dance performance entitled, "The Anguish of Modern Existence." He performed at "underground" theatres, art cafés, modern art museums, retirement homes, birthday parties, restaurant openings, and anywhere that he could find people willing to pay to watch this sort of thing. He even performed for free at local parks as a way of "giving back" to the community.

When he came back he was quite changed. He wore his Princeton Interpretive Dance Varsity jacket with more attitude and to any occasion; he wore it when working out, going to sleep, playing tennis, and I even saw him wearing it while swimming. He switched from the glass jar of Beige Poupon to the squeeze bottle and would often demonstrate its revolutionary squeeze technique. Sometimes, he didn't even say, "thank you." He was more enthusiastic about dance than ever and his annoyance meter was now off the scale. There were actually people who liked his performance. I know, it's crazy to think so but it's kind of like how someone wants to marry a serial killer in prison. No matter how insane you think it is, there is someone out there with enough of a warped brain to enjoy it.

But all of this went to his head—and his head was already huge to begin with. Especially when women gave him attention. I mean, how can you forget a grown man in an all-black body suit crying while attempting to act like a swan in an interpretation of the "Lost Generation?" Must have triggered some long repressed maternal instinct. That is when and where Frances lost him. Although, I have to say, it would have been better off had she not found him in the first place. And if you did find something like that, why would you hang onto him? Oh right, the serial killer syndrome.

I mean, for years, he had never seen beyond Frances and Poopsy-Pops. I am sure he had never been in love in his life—unless you count his relationship with Beige Poupon, which bordered on obsessive. But now he realized that there were women who wanted to live with him—it was not simply a divine miracle. This changed him in ways only a narcissist could change.

He also kept winning when we played Uno. It made him rather vain, and he talked several times about how he, and only he, could always make a living at Uno if he were ever forced to. Because clearly, professional Uno playing was the logical next step after interpretive dance champion.

Then there was another thing. He had gotten addicted to silent movies. That sounds like an innocent occupation, but Cohn had seen and re-seen a silent film about Ratty Rat.

Ratty Rat was a cartoon rat that whistled and sang about true friendships, following your dreams, and everything else you'd expect from a motivational cartoon character. Most people loved it, but I couldn't stand it.

This particular Ratty Rat movie is very influential if watched too late in life by someone with too much money and too little sense. It featured splendid imaginary adventures of a cartoon rat in a magical land.

Cohn, I believe, took every frame of that Ratty Rat film as literally as though it had been a documentary. You understand me, he made some reservations, but overall the film to him was a blueprint for happiness. I did not realize the extent to which it had impacted him until one day when he came into my office, wearing a navy blazer with brass buttons and carrying a small picnic basket that undoubtedly contained Beige Poupon and Poopsy-Pops's afternoon snacks.

"Hello, Robert," I said. "Did you watch that movie again today?"

"Only three times today. It's very insightful."

He stood there waiting for me to agree with him. I could see he had something on his mind, and knowing Cohn, there was no avoiding it. I sighed and put down my papers.

"Would you like to go to Rattyland, Jake?" he asked.

"No."

"Why not?"

"I don't know. It doesn't exist. You do realize we are in the 1920s here, right? In addition, even if it did exist it would be too crowded for me to enjoy it. Also, you can see all the cartoon rats you want in Paris anyway."

"They're not the real Ratty Rat."

"Robert, Ratty Rat isn't real either."

At this point, Cohn started humming under his breath: "R-A-T... talk to you real soon... T-Y... why? Because I love you..."

"Listen," I said, desperate to change the subject, "I'm planning a trip to Spain this summer for the rooster fights. You know, the Running of the Roosters? I hear they've been sharpening those beaks for months now. Want to come?"

Cohn completely ignored my invitation, which was great because I was beating myself up as soon as I said it.

"But all my life I've wanted to go on a trip to Rattyland," Cohn said. He sat down pouting and pulled out his Beige Poupon, spreading it absent-mindedly on a dinner roll he'd apparently been carrying in his blazer pocket. "I'll be too old before I can ever do it."

"Don't be a fool," I said. "You'll most likely be dead before Rattyland is even built, especially considering how we drink. But you've got plenty of money. Why don't you go someplace that is real and stop getting your inspirations from cartoons."

"I know. But I can't get it out of my mind." He started singing again, more desperately this time: "R-A-T-T-Y R-A-T..."

"Cheer up," I said. "Even when it's built it will be a park made of cheap plastic, smelly waiting lines, and overpriced food."

But I felt sorry for him. He was addicted. I should have known it would be like this. He jumps from one idea to another and is unable to let anything go.

He sighed and said, "I can't stand it to think my life is going so fast and I'm not really living it."

"Nobody ever lives their life all the way up except rooster fighters."

"I'm not interested in rooster fighters. That's an abnormal life, dodging those razor-sharp beaks. I want to go to Rattyland." He was now quietly humming the Ratty Rat song again, which was somehow more disturbing than when he sang it loudly. He was completely delusional. How did I ever get myself mixed up with this guy anyway? At this point there was only one thing that I could think of to say.

"Come on down-stairs and have a drink."

"Aren't you working?"

"How can I with you going on about someplace that doesn't even exist?" I said. We went down the stairs to the café on the ground floor. I had discovered that was the best way to get rid of friends, especially ones who wanted to visit fictional locations. Once you had a drink all you had to say was: "Well, I've got to get back to work," and it was done.

Anyway, we went downstairs to the bar and had a whiskey and soda. And why wouldn't we? It's noon on a workday in the 1920s so let's just drink some hard alcohol. Cohn looked at the bottles in bins around the wall while methodically applying Beige Poupon to some crackers he'd found.

"This is a good place. Look at all this liquor," he said.

"It's true and over the course of this book we'll be drinking most of it," I agreed.

"Listen, Jake," he said as he leaned forward on the bar, leaving Beige Poupon fingerprints on the mahogany. "Don't you ever get the feeling that all your life is going by and you're not taking advantage of it? Do you realize you've lived nearly half the time you have to live already?"

"Yes, every once in a while."

"Well, I want to go to Rattyland." He started humming again and then finished the song: "...see you real soon, T-Y, why? Because I love you…"

"Listen, Robert, going to any theme park doesn't make any difference. I've tried all that. You can't get away from yourself by paying money to live in a fantasy world. There's nothing to that. Especially when the place doesn't actually exist."

"I'm sick of Paris, and I'm sick of the Quarter."

So, there you were. I was sorry for him, but there was nothing I could do about it. He had created two walls of stubbornness: Rattyland could fix it and he did not like Paris. He got the first idea from watching too many cartoons, and I suppose the second came out of excessive Beige Poupon consumption affecting his brain.

"Well," I said, "I've got to go upstairs and get some work done."

"Do you really have to go?"

"Yes, because unlike you I have a real job."

"Do you mind if I come up and sit around the office?"

I rolled my eyes and sighed, "I guess, if you really have nothing better to do and want to watch me work."

He sat in the outer room and colored a Ratty Rat coloring book while I worked. Eventually, I went out into the other room and there was Robert Cohn asleep in the big chair. He was asleep with his head on his arms, and I could hear him singing softly in his sleep: "R-A-T... talk to you real soon..."

I did not want to wake him up, but I wanted to lock the office and go home or to the café. I put my hand on his shoulder. He shook his head. "He won't let me," he said, and put his head deeper into his arms. "He won't let me! Ratty won't let me into the Cheesy Kingdom!"

"Robert," I said, and shook him by the shoulder. He looked up. He smiled and blinked.

"Did I talk out loud just then?"

"Something about Ratty Rat. But it wasn't clear."

"I didn't sleep all last night."

"What was the matter?"

"Talking," he said. "Frances kept asking me why I was humming cartoon songs and questioning if I made eye contact with any girls that day."

I could picture it. I have a rotten habit of picturing the bedroom scenes of my friends, especially when they involve tiny dogs and cartoon rat-related arguments. I shuddered.

We went out to the Café Drunk Napoleon to have their signature drink, "The Waterloo" and watch the evening crowd on the Boulevard. Cohn ordered his drink and then pulled his Beige Poupon out of his pocket, naturally.

Chapter 3: Mimes and Pretending Yoga is Deep

It was a warm spring night and I sat at a table on the terrace of the Café Drunk Napoleon after Robert had gone, watching the sky darken and the electric signs come on.

I didn't come here for this reason (I promise), but this area is a common spot for women of the night. I watched several walk past my table but I knew what I was looking for. And then I found her. A good-looking girl walked past the table and came back again. She was dressed in black pants with a black and white striped shirt. She was walking against an invisible wind, then seemed to be trapped behind some kind of invisible wall, pressing her hands against it in distress.

Finally. A classic Paris mime.

She caught my eye and came over, still trapped in her invisible box, and sat down at the table. The waiter came up.

"Well, what will you drink?" I asked.

She held up her hands and began miming drinking something. First, she pretended to open a bottle, then pour it into an invisible glass, then sip it delicately. It was either wine or she was having a very elaborate seizure.

"Well," I said to the waiter, "whatever she's pretending to drink."

The waiter looked confused. "Monsieur?"

"Just bring us two wines."

The mime began an elaborate routine of being delighted with her imaginary beverage, clapping silently and doing a little dance in her chair.

"So," I said, "how about some dinner?"

She grinned and started miming eating. First, she cut an invisible steak, then twirled invisible pasta, then ate an invisible apple. Watching someone eat nothing while you're trying to have a conversation is surprisingly depressing.

"I'll take that as a yes."

We walked to a restaurant, where she continued her invisible meal routine. The waiter kept asking if she wanted to actually order food, but she just kept chewing air and patting her stomach contentedly. I ordered for both of us and watched her pretend to eat a seven-course meal while her real food sat untouched.

Just then from the other room someone called: "Barnes! I say, Barnes! Jacob Barnes!"

"It's a friend calling me," I explained to the mime, who responded by pretending to be sad that I was leaving, wiping away invisible tears.

It was Braddocks at a big table with a party: Cohn, Frances Clyne, Mrs. Braddocks, and Poopsy-Pops in a tiny highchair eating what appeared to be caviar.

"You're coming to the hot yoga session, aren't you?" Braddocks asked.

"What hot yoga session?"

"The one at the new hot yoga studio, 'Painful Pose.' Haven't you done it before?" Mrs. Braddocks asked while fanning herself with a menu. "It's supposed to center your chakras."

"You must come, Jake. We're all going to get in touch with the universe," Frances said from the end of the table, while feeding Poopsy-Pops tiny spoonfuls of pâté.

"Of course, he'll be there," Braddocks said. "But first, come in and have coffee with us, Barnes."

"And bring your friend," said Mrs. Braddocks. "Though I'm not sure how she'll manage the poses if she's stuck in that box."

I went back to the mime, who was now pretending to be full and patting her invisible belly.

"We're going to do hot yoga with the others," I said.

She looked thrilled and began demonstrating yoga poses, or possibly having some kind of fit. It was hard to tell.

We went into the room full of people and Braddocks and Cohn stood up.

"I wish to present Mademoiselle… uh… mime." I realized I had no idea what her name was, since she'd never spoken.

The mime then began an elaborate charade, pointing to herself and acting out letters. After several minutes of interpretive alphabet, we found out her name was Georgette.

After coffee, we all went to the hot yoga studio. The studio was a converted wine cellar in the Rue de la Montagne Sainte Geneviève, heated to approximately the temperature of hell. Five nights a week, wealthy people came here to "find themselves" while sweating profusely and telling others how great it made them feel both physically and mentally.

All my friends brought their designer water bottles, some were diamond-encrusted with their names. They boasted about the material their bottle was made from and how it was better than anything else out there. In their minds they thought sweating and drinking water for one night would compensate for drinking every night until two in the morning.

I looked at Cohn's water bottle: it was a kid's Ratty Rat thermos with what appeared to be a gold nameplate attached to it. The plate read, 'Princeton Dance Champion: Past, Present, and Future.' It also had a carabiner clip attached.

"What's up with your water bottle?" I asked Cohn.

"I knew you'd appreciate it," he said proudly. "I had it customized for my body's specific hydration requirements. The clip enables me to stay hydrated no matter what difficult routine I'm performing. It's a completely revolutionary invention I call 'Portable Hydration.'"

"You mean… a water bottle with a clip?"

"No, no, you don't understand. This is *portable hydration.* I'm thinking of patenting it."

I looked over at Braddocks who was stretching against the wall.

"I wish people would come earlier," Braddocks said, mopping his forehead. "The heat isn't properly distributed yet."

A yoga instructor appeared and began demonstrating poses while everyone pretended this was normal instead of just uncomfortable. As the instructor began to demonstrate a pose I left to get some water. It was very hot and the chanting music was giving me a headache. I stood in the doorway getting cool air from the street when two taxis came down the steep street.

A crowd of young men got out, all wearing matching yoga outfits and carrying designer water bottles. I could see their perfectly coiffed hair and manicured hands in the light from the door. With them was Brett.

And then something extraordinary happened. As Brett walked under the light, three people on the street literally fainted by looking at her. Just dropped. A waiter carrying a tray of drinks stopped mid-step, stared at her, and walked directly into a lamppost. A small dog started howling. Brett was the most beautiful person I had ever seen and completely oblivious to the chaos her appearance was causing.

One of the men who was with Brett saw the mime and said: "Wow! An actual mime. I'm going to ask her to teach me the trapped-in-a-box pose."

I was getting annoyed. These yoga enthusiasts always made me angry with their superior attitudes about "finding inner peace" while spending more on workout clothes than most people made in a month.

When I came back inside, there was a crowd on the yoga mats so I made my way to a nearby table and sat down. Cohn was sitting there holding Poopsy-Pops, and when Brett walked by, something happened to him that I can only describe as a complete system shutdown. His mouth fell open. I mean, it literally fell open—I could see his tonsils. Then he started drooling. Not a little drool. A steady stream, like a broken faucet.

Frances, busy adjusting Poopsy-Pops's tiny yoga outfit, didn't notice at first. When she looked up and saw Cohn's condition, she followed his gaze to Brett and her face went completely white.

"Robert," she hissed. "Robert, you're drooling on Poopsy-Pops."

Cohn didn't respond. He was making a low humming sound—not the Ratty Rat song this time, just a general noise of appreciation. It was deeply disturbing.

Mrs. Braddocks brought up somebody and introduced him as Robert Prentiss, a rising new novelist who'd just discovered hot yoga and wouldn't shut up about it.

"The heat really opens your creative channels," he was saying. "I've written seventeen pages today just from the spiritual clarity."

He was still talking to me as I got up and walked toward Brett, who was at the water station.

"Hello, Jake. I haven't seen you around lately."

"Hello, Brett," I said. "Why aren't you doing yoga?"

"I was getting too sweaty."

She stood holding her water bottle, skin glistening from the heat, and I saw Cohn still staring at her with that disturbing drool situation. He looked like he was planning to follow her home. Which, knowing Cohn, he probably was.

Brett was very attractive. She was from England and had a cool English accent. She wore yoga pants and a sports top, and her hair was pulled back in a perfect ponytail. Even in workout clothes, she looked like she'd stepped off a magazine cover.

Another person walking by glanced at her and promptly tripped over their yoga mat.

I'd known Brett since the war. She was a nurse at the hospital they sent me to. She had a particular talent for turning ordinary evenings into chaos. We'd been through this dance before—the dramatic entrances, the trail of mesmerized men, the inevitable complications. Every time I told myself I wouldn't get pulled back in, and every time I found myself right back where I started. I had to admit it, she was my ultimate crush.

"Interesting group that you're with this time, Brett," I said.

"Aren't they lovely? All very spiritually centered. And you, my dear. Where did you get the mime?"

"At the Café Drunk Napoleon."

"And have you had a lovely evening of silent communication?"

"Oh, priceless," I said.

The yoga instructor started a new session and Cohn managed to close his mouth long enough to say: "Will you do partner poses with me, Lady Brett?"

Brett smiled at him, which caused him to start drooling again. "I've promised to do partner poses with Jake," she said. "Though I have to warn you, I'm terrible at this yoga nonsense."

"How about the next session?" asked Cohn.

"We're leaving," Brett said. "We're going out for drinks at the Les Miserabeers."

During our halfhearted attempt at yoga poses, I could see Cohn in the corner, still watching Brett.

"You've made a new stalker there," I said to her. "We might need to leave because I'm sure he's just waiting for you to do some pose that requires you to bend over or something."

"Gross. Don't talk about it. I could hear him breathing heavily from across the room."

"Oh, well," I said. "I suppose you like to collect them."

"I do not!"

"You do."

"What if I do? And what's up with this Cohn guy anyway. Is he wealthy or anything like that?"

I rolled my eyes. Typical Brett. We finished the yoga session and I got my jacket. Brett stood by the water station. Cohn was talking to her, or rather, standing near her making incoherent sounds while she politely nodded.

We started out the door. "Good night, Robert," I said. He was still making that humming noise. Outside in the street we looked for a taxi.

"That man is going to follow me home, isn't he?" Brett said.

"Most likely. He follows me home sometimes too."

"Wonderful."

"Come on, let's get a drink in the pub next door."

We went into the next bar. We sat by the window and ordered our drinks. Once the drinks came we raised our glasses and as they got close to touching we were jolted by a loud noise outside. We both screamed, spilling most of our drinks. It was Cohn, he had tripped and slammed his face into the window as he was watching us.

"Ok," I said, "we're out of here. Let's get a taxi."

We walked outside and I hailed a taxi. Brett pressed my hand hard as it pulled up. Once we got in, she leaned back in the corner.

"Oh, darling, I've been so miserable," Brett said.

And here we go again, I thought. *Here we go again.* This is what always happens with Brett. She shows up out of nowhere looking like a goddess, causes half the city to have nervous breakdowns, collects a few more admirers, and then suddenly she's "miserable" about something completely ridiculous.

"Let me guess," I said. "What is it this time? Did your maid quit? Did the store run out of your favorite champagne? Did someone buy the same dress as you?"

"No, darling, it's much worse than that," she said seriously. "I've only met five new rich men this week. Five! Last week I met eight. I'm clearly losing my touch. What if I'm becoming ordinary? What if I have to start having actual conversations with people instead of just standing there being beautiful?"

I stared at her. "Brett, three people fainted when you walked into that yoga studio tonight."

"Did they? I hadn't noticed. But still, only five new men this week. It's practically a tragedy."

I looked out the window at Paris rolling by and wondered how I always ended up in these situations. Here I was, a man with a serious war injury that we were never supposed to talk about but that we will keep bringing up. It was an unfortunate and debilitating case of toe fungus that prevented me from having normal relationships. I simply stepped in the wrong puddle on the Italian front. And here I was listening to a woman who loved feet, who couldn't live with anyone who had less than perfect feet, complain about having too few millionaires falling at her feet.

"You're right," I said. "That is truly miserable."

But even as I said it, I knew I'd be right back here again next week, listening to Brett's latest crisis about being too beautiful or too wealthy or too admired. Because that's what we do in Paris. We drink, we complain about our impossible lives, and we pretend it's all very deep and meaningful.

As the taxi continued away into the Parisian night, I realized that meeting Brett had only complicated my life in ways I couldn't yet imagine. At least with the mime I didn't have to hear her complain.

Chapter 4: Count Cholesterol and Foot Remedies

The taxi went up the hill, passed the lighted square, then on into the dark, still climbing. We were sitting apart and we jolted close together going down the old street. Brett's hat was off. Her head was back. I saw her face in the lights from the open shops, then it was dark, then I saw her face clearly as we came out on the Avenue des Gobelins.

"I can't stand it," Brett said suddenly as I leaned closer. "I can't stand it."

"What's the matter?"

"Your condition, I can't stand it."

"Oh, Brett. Don't you love me?"

She was sitting up now, trying to look into my eyes and fighting not to look down at my foot. I could see beads of sweat appear on her brow. Her face started twitching.

"And there's nothing we could do," I said.

"You know," Brett said, not looking at me, "I went to podiatry school once. Thought I could help people with foot problems. But I dropped out the first week when they showed us a case of severe toe fungus. I couldn't handle it. Just couldn't. The irony is killing me."

"Brett—"

"And then there's the money thing. Jake, darling, you simply don't make enough. I need someone who can afford my lifestyle. Someone who can buy me things and take me places."

She looked out the window and sighed before she continued, "I remember when I first heard about you in the hospital, everyone was talking about this American who was going to get a substantial government settlement for his unique war injury. I thought, 'How interesting—a wounded hero with a guaranteed income.' I had no idea it would turn out to be such a modest arrangement. And then—"

I was starting to feel the familiar burning sensation in my feet. "Brett, I think I need to—"

"Oh no, you know the drill," she said, rolling down the taxi window. "Foot, out! Quick!"

I stuck my foot out the window into the cool night air. The relief was immediate but humiliating.

Just then, another taxi pulled up right beside us at a red light. I looked over and there was Robert Cohn, pressed against the window, staring at us with his mouth hanging open. He was straining to look around me to get a better view of Brett.

"Is that Cohn?" Brett asked, following my gaze.

Cohn waved enthusiastically and started miming something through his taxi window. It looked like he was asking if we needed medical attention, or possibly if he could join us for whatever foot-related activity he thought we were engaged in.

"Drive faster," I told our driver.

"Where do you want to go?" I asked Brett, pulling my foot back in as we sped away from Cohn's taxi.

"Oh, go to the Reject."

"Café Reject," I told the driver. "Boulevard Montparnasse."

When the taxi stopped I got out and paid. Brett came out putting on her hat. A big sign above the Café read, "Café Reject: Rejecting Reality One Drink at a Time."

Inside, against the bar and at tables, were most of the crowd who had been at the hot yoga session. As soon as we walked inside we almost tripped over the smallest man in Paris. He came out of nowhere. What was this guy doing, waiting in the corner for Brett? And how did he know she was even going to be here? She has literally created a stalker on every block.

"Whoa, little guy!" I said.

"Oh, Brett! Brett!" the little Greek portrait-painter, who called himself a duke, ran up to her. "I got something to tell you."

"Hello, Zizi," Brett said.

"I want you to meet a friend," Zizi said. Then he gestured toward another doorway.

Trumpets blew and we both flinched. Out of nowhere a loud voice boomed, "Presenting His Royal Roundness, Owner and CEO of The Count's Heart-Stoppin' Chicken restaurants, Count Cholesterol." We then heard heavy breathing and what sounded like someone trying to squeeze through a space too small for them. A distinct smell of fried chicken overwhelmed the room. Two waiters appeared, pushing against what I can only describe as the largest human being I had ever seen. Count Cholesterol was so enormous that he was literally stuck in the doorway of the café.

"Push harder!" he wheezed from somewhere in the doorway. "I can almost… just a little more…"

Finally, with a loud pop, he came through, stumbling forward and nearly crushing Zizi. He was sweating profusely and had to lean against the bar to catch his breath.

"Count Cholesterol, meet my friend Lady Ashley," Zizi said.

"How do you do?" said Brett, and I could practically see the dollar signs appear in her eyes as she took in his diamond-encrusted watch, his solid gold walking stick, and the way everyone in the café immediately started fawning over him. The only thing larger than him was his wallet.

"Well," he panted, still trying to catch his breath, "does your Ladyship… like it here… here in Paris?" He paused between every few words to breathe.

"Rather," said Brett, now fully focused on him with laser-like intensity.

"Paris is… a fine town… all right," said the count, mopping his forehead with what appeared to be a silk handkerchief. "But I guess… you have pretty big… doings yourself… over in London."

"Oh, yes," said Brett. "But let's talk more about you. What kind of business do you do? How many yachts do you own…."

I could see this was going exactly where I thought it would. Brett was already positioning herself closer to the count. I had had enough. I started to say good night to Brett at the bar. The count was ordering champagne, which required him to point at the bottle since he was too winded to speak.

"Will you take a glass of wine with us, sir?" he managed to ask between breaths.

"No, thank you. I have to go."

"Really going?" Brett asked, though she was clearly more interested in Count Cholesterol's wallet than my departure.

"Yes," I said. "I've got a rotten headache."

"Why don't we meet at the Pretentious tomorrow? I know there is no way that I will get too drunk to remember and forget that I promised to meet you there."

"I'm sure. Either way, I'll be there at five."

I went out onto the sidewalk and walked home, passing the crowded tables where people were spending more on a single bottle of wine than I made in a week. Someone waved at me from a table, but I didn't see who it was and went on. I wanted to get home, get my feet into a comfortable position, and stop thinking about Brett and her newfound fascination with Count Cholesterol's obvious wealth.

Back in my room, I looked at my mail. There was a bank statement showing I had $1,832.60, which was barely enough to keep me afloat, let alone compete with someone who could afford to get stuck in doorways because he owned too many businesses to count.

I got into my Pokémon pajamas and sat on the bed with a pint of ice cream and the latest medical journal I'd ordered from South America. There was an article about experimental toe fungus treatments being developed in Brazil, involving some kind of tree bark extract. I ate ice cream and read about potential cures for my condition, which seemed both pathetic and necessary.

"Revolutionary Treatment for Persistent Toe Fungus Shows Promise in Amazon Trials," read one headline. I spooned more ice cream into my mouth and read about how researchers had found a fungus-eating fungus that could potentially cure cases like mine. The article went on to state that so far only 50% of the study participants had died during the research. "Not too shabby. Better odds than me dating Brett," I said to myself.

I then dropped some ice cream on my new Pokémon PJ's, right on Pikachu, caught a glance of myself in the mirror, and I started to cry. Here I was, a grown man eating ice cream in bed while reading medical journals about foot diseases. Meanwhile, the woman I loved was probably falling for the fattest, richest man in Paris. It was absurd and miserable and perfectly fitting for my life. And I "loved" her, right? I mean, it wasn't just because she looked great in yoga pants. I was looking deeper. Oh, who am I kidding? I'm as shallow as everyone else.

I lay in bed counting Pokémon cards in my head and eventually went to sleep, still holding the medical journal.

I finally settled down and was having the best dream of my life. Pikachu had learned a new move and was just about to electrocute my toe fungus away when I awoke to the sound of Brett's voice outside. She was stumbling around yelling my name over and over again. *How do I get myself mixed up with these people?* I thought.

Brett came up the stairs. I saw she was quite drunk and looked disheveled. "I say, you weren't asleep, were you?" she said.

"Of course I was asleep. Don't you know what time it is? You know, some of us actually have a job."

I looked at the clock. It was half-past four.

"Had no idea what hour it was," Brett said. "Don't be mad, darling. Just left the count. He brought me here. Why don't you pour us a drink?"

"Are you serious?" I asked. "It's four in the morning, you're still completely drunk and you want another drink? Plus, I just woke up, if I drink now I'll probably puke."

"Don't you know we are the "Lost Generation?" This is what we do, honey. We drink copious amounts of alcohol at any time, day or night. We then complain about our lives and wonder what is wrong. It's what this book is all about, don't you understand? At least it was what the classic book was all about. Not this butchered nonsense."

She had a point. I poured us each a brandy and soda.

"What's the count like?" I asked.

"The count? He's quite something. Owns multiple businesses—the largest is a chain of fried chicken restaurants in the States."

She sipped at her glass.

"Hundreds of them. All across America. Makes an absolute fortune. Very interesting, really."

She took another drink.

"Where did you go with him?"

"Oh, everywhere. He even bought me this diamond bracelet. He just brought me here now. Had to help him get out of the car, mind you. Takes three people to get him mobile."

Brett laughed.

She looked at me, her hand on the table. "Don't look like that," she said. "Told him I love you. True, too."

My heart fluttered. She loved me. I thought now was the time to tell her about those experimental treatments in South America. But before I could even start to explain Brett tilted her head back and drained her drink like a college student at a sorority party.

"Love you because you're such a great friend," she said.

And there you have it. ***The friend zone***.

"Just wanted to see you," she continued. "Silly idea. Want to get dressed and come down? He's got the car just up the street. Had to get a specially reinforced one, you know."

"The count?"

"Himself. And two chauffeurs to help him get in and out. Going to drive me around and have breakfast in the Bois. Then shopping, bottles of champagne, a spa treatment, and even more shopping. Tempt you?"

"So, you basically woke me up at four in the morning to tell me how great the Count is and how much fun you're going to have with him and his wallet."

"Absolutely."

"That's great. Good night, Brett."

"Don't be sentimental."

"You make me ill."

I went back upstairs and from the open window watched Brett walking up the street to an enormous limousine. It took two chauffeurs and Brett herself to help Count Cholesterol get situated in the back seat. The car visibly sagged under his weight.

I turned around. On the table was my melted ice cream and the medical journal still open to the article about toe fungus cures. I closed the journal, threw away the ice cream container, and got into bed.

This was the real Brett. I shook my head at myself for any tears I've spent because of her; at that moment, I gave up hope for anything between the two of us. She was off with the fattest, richest man in Paris, while I sat in the friend zone alone, reading about experimental foot treatments. It's easy not to be bothered about everything in the daytime, but at night it is another thing. Especially when your feet itch and the woman you love is attracted to men who own fried chicken empires.

Chapter 5: Cohn's Unitard and the Curse Revealed

In the morning I walked down the Boulevard to the rue Soufflot for coffee and brioche. It was a calm morning. The horse-chestnut trees in the Luxembourg gardens were in bloom. There was the pleasant early morning feeling of a hot day. I sat outside and read a newspaper in the warm sunlight. After a while I stood up and began to make my way to work. I felt good and relaxed; I was happy to be walking to work.

I walked across the avenue known for toy sellers. They would line up along the street showcasing their latest toys. I passed a man with jumping frog toys and a man with boxer toys. I felt at peace until I heard a commotion behind me.

"Jake! Jake! Wait up!"

I turned to see Cohn running toward me, wearing what appeared to be a full-body black dance unitard. He was carrying Poopsy-Pops in one arm and had a small jar of Beige Poupon tucked under the other. As he ran, he somehow managed to trip over the rope controlling the jumping frogs, sending them flying in all directions.

"Sorry!" he called to the vendor but didn't stop running.

Next, he crashed directly into the man with the boxer toys, sending the little wooden fighters scattering across the sidewalk. Children who had been watching the demonstration immediately started crying as their entertainment was destroyed under Cohn's desperate sprint.

"Excusez-moi!" Cohn yelled, still not stopping, while Poopsy-Pops yapped frantically from his arms.

The toy vendors stared at him in disbelief as this grown man in a skin-tight dance outfit destroyed their morning's work. One vendor began shouting in rapid French while shaking his fist, but Cohn was already past him, leaving a trail of broken toys and crying children in his wake.

"Jake!" he panted as he finally caught up to me. "I've been looking everywhere for you!"

"What are you wearing and why?" I asked.

"Oh, this?" He looked down at his unitard. "I had an early morning interpretive dance performance at the Sorbonne. 'The Anguish of Academic Pursuit.' It didn't go very well. They cancelled all further shows. I was going to play tennis but I haven't won a game in days, even tried to beat someone's grandma but failed. I haven't been winning at Uno either. I don't know what's going on."

Poopsy-Pops was still trembling from the run and making little whimpering sounds.

"Robert, you just destroyed half the street vendors' inventory."

"Did I? Oh." He looked back at the chaos he'd created with complete indifference. "Jake, I need to talk to you. It's important. Do you want to get something to eat?"

I looked at this man in his ridiculous outfit, holding a terrified Pomeranian, having just traumatized several children, acting like nothing had happened because he wanted to discuss whatever was on his mind.

"Fine," I said. "Let's eat."

We went to a restaurant with outdoor seating so Poopsy-Pops could join us. Cohn had changed into his regular clothes but still had that post-performance glow that comes from making a complete fool of yourself in public.

In the restaurant we ordered hors d'œuvres and beer. Why beer? Because it's mandated to drink in each chapter of this book—it's what we do. Cohn immediately began hand-feeding tiny pieces of pâté to Poopsy-Pops while nervously glancing around.

"Frances doesn't know I'm here," he said quietly. "She thinks I'm at home working on my… my dance routine."

"How's the new routine going?"

"Not good. Nothing seems to work. It's supposed to be about 'The Futility of Modern Romance' but it just looks like I'm having some kind of seizure."

"That happens to everybody."

"Jake," he said, lowering his voice and feeding Poopsy-Pops another morsel, "have you given any more thought to Rattyland?"

"Robert, we've been through this. It doesn't exist."

"But when it does exist, do you think… do you think Lady Brett would want to go there with me?"

I stared at him. Here it was. The real reason for this entire conversation, the destruction of the toy vendors, the ridiculous outfit, and the nervous Poopsy-Pops feeding.

"What do you know about Lady Brett Ashley, Jake?" he asked, still glancing around nervously for Frances.

"Her name's Lady Ashley. Brett's her own name. She's getting a divorce and she's going to marry Mike Campbell. He's over in Scotland now. Why?"

"She's a remarkably attractive woman."

"Isn't she?"

"There's a certain quality about her, a certain fineness. Do you think she likes Ratty Rat?"

I nearly choked on my beer. "What?"

"Ratty Rat. Do you think she'd enjoy the Cheesy Magic Kingdom? Maybe we could sing the song together. 'R-A-T…'"

"Robert, stop."

"There's something about her," Cohn continued, feeding Poopsy-Pops while humming softly. "I suppose it's breeding. Do you think she has good breeding?"

"Good breeding? What are you talking about?"

"I think I'm in love with her. Do you think she'd like to go to Rattyland when it's built? We could ride the teacups together."

I put down my beer. "She's a drunk," I said. "She's in love with Mike Campbell, and she's going to marry him. He's going to be as rich as the count someday. Also, she hates Ratty. Absolutely despises everything about Ratty Rat. Can't stand the songs, the characters, the whole concept. Makes her physically ill."

Cohn's face went white. Poopsy-Pops sensed the change in mood and started whimpering.

"I don't believe that," he said.

"Why not?"

"I don't know. I just don't believe it. She seems like someone who would appreciate the magic."

"Robert, yesterday she told me that if she ever heard the Ratty Rat Club song again, she might commit violence. She then specifically mentioned interpretive dance as something that should be banned."

"You're lying."

"She also said that anyone who spreads Beige Poupon on *anything* should be deported."

Cohn looked down at the Beige Poupon he'd been spreading on his bread and his face wrinkled.

"You're just bitter because of your little toe situation over there," he said, wagging his finger in the direction of my feet.

"Sorry. I was just trying to give you the facts."

"I don't believe it."

"Well," I said, "don't ask me a lot of stupid questions if you don't like the answers."

He stood up from the table, his face white, still holding Poopsy-Pops. The little dog looked terrified by the sudden movement.

"Sit down," I said. "Don't get crazy."

"You've got to take that back."

"Oh, cut out the prep-school stuff."

"Take it back. About Brett hating Ratty."

"Sure. Anything. Brett loves Ratty Rat. She wants to move to Rattyland and live in Ratty's Cheese Castle. How's that?"

Cohn looked down at the trembling Pomeranian and sat down. He seemed glad to sit down. What would he have done if he hadn't sat down? Challenge me to an interpretive dance battle?

"You say some very insulting things, Jake."

"I'm sorry. I've got a nasty tongue. I never mean it when I say nasty things." Although I clearly meant it in this case.

"I know it," Cohn said. "You're really about the best friend I have, Jake."

I almost choked on my beer again. *What a loser*, I thought.

"Forget what I said," I said out loud. "I'm sorry."

"It's all right. It's fine. I was just sore for a minute." He started humming the Ratty Rat song under his breath while feeding Poopsy-Pops. "Do you really think she hates Ratty?"

"Robert."

"Right. Sorry. Let's go get some coffee."

After we finished the lunch, Cohn carefully placed Poopsy-Pops back in her carrier bag and we walked to a café for coffee. I could feel Cohn wanted to bring up Brett and Rattyland again, but I held him off it. We talked about his morning performance (apparently everyone had walked out), his latest Beige Poupon experiments (he was trying it on ice cream), and his concern that Frances was getting suspicious of his Brett obsession.

When I left him to go back to the office, he was still sitting there, humming the Ratty Rat song and staring off into the distance, probably imagining Brett in rat ears.

I felt sorry for him, but there was nothing I could do. The man was living in a fantasy world where a beautiful, wealthy, alcoholic woman would want to visit an imaginary theme park with a grown man who performed interpretive dance in a unitard while carrying around someone else's tiny dog.

I also realized that since he had met Brett nothing had gone right for him. He had admitted he couldn't win at tennis or Uno, two things he always excelled at. His new show was cancelled, and he was having issues putting together a new routine. Probably just a coincidence, but then again, this was Brett.

I began to think about her last two boyfriends. There was Fabio Gustavo, a famous model who after meeting Brett was horribly disfigured in a freak explosion while modeling flame resistant underwear. Then came Paul Weinstein, a famous stock trader from New York. He went bankrupt putting everything into a company that turned out to be nothing more than one guy and a hot dog cart. The list of disasters went on and on for as long as I've known her. How could all of this be a coincidence?

I started wondering if there were such things as curses. And if so, what was my curse? Technically, I never dated Brett but all I knew was with friends like this, how could anyone say I wasn't cursed.

Chapter 6: Vampire Harvey and Frances Unhinged

At five o'clock I was in the Hotel Pretentious waiting for Brett. Not surprisingly she did not turn up, so about quarter to six I went down to the bar and had a Jack Rose with George the barman. This turned out to be the best decision I'd made all week. Within minutes, I'd met another group of Americans who were in Paris doing something vaguely artistic and completely funded by their families. They seemed more normal than my group of Americans who were in Paris doing vaguely artistic things completely funded by their families.

"You simply must join us later," said a woman named Vivian who claimed to be a sculptor but was clearly just very wealthy. "We're going to Le Macabre for the evening show."

"What's Le Macabre?" I asked.

"Oh, it's this marvelous gothic café where they serve drinks in skull mugs and have the most authentic vampire performances. Much more genuine than those tourist traps."

This sounded infinitely more entertaining than waiting around for Brett to remember she had promised to meet me.

"I'll see you there," I said, and took a taxi toward Montparnasse.

The taxi stopped in front of what used to be the Rotonde but was now called "Le Macabre." The entire front had been painted black, with fake gargoyles perched above the entrance. A sign read: "Le Macabre: Where We Enjoy Depression."

There were indeed skull-shaped mugs visible through the windows, and I could hear dramatic organ music playing inside.

Outside, alone at a table, sat Harvey Stone. I had known Harvey for years. He had a collection of skull mugs in front of him which was his way of counting and boasting about how much he drank. He was dressed entirely in black, including a cape, and looked like he hadn't seen sunlight in months.

"Ah, Jacob," he said in an overly dramatic Transylvanian accent. "I have been expecting you."

"Hello, Harvey. How's the... uh... vampire thing going?"

"It is not a 'thing,'" he said dramatically. "It is an authentic expression of the darkness that dwells within the human soul. Unlike some people's pathetic attempts at artistic expression."

Harvey had apparently undergone a complete transformation since I'd last seen him. Gone was the somewhat normal American expatriate artist. In his place sat someone who looked like he'd stepped out of a gothic novel.

"I haven't had anything to eat for five days," he announced. "I sustain myself only on the essence of artistic suffering."

"What's the matter?"

"Nothing is the matter. Everything is as it should be. I am embracing the authentic darkness of existence, not like some people who prance around in unitards pretending to express deep emotions through interpretive dance."

"Are you talking about Cohn?"

"That pretender! That fraud! His so-called 'art' is nothing but popular garbage designed to appeal to the masses. True artistic expression comes from genuine suffering, from embracing the void, not from spreading condiments on bread and humming cartoon songs."

As if summoned by Harvey's disdain, Robert Cohn appeared, crossing the street. He was wearing his cream cable-knit sweater and carrying Poopsy-Pops in her designer carrier.

"That moron," said Harvey, his fake accent slipping slightly.

"Hello, you bums," Cohn said cheerfully as he approached our table.

"Ah, the dancing fool arrives," Harvey said, back in full gothic mode. "Tell me, Robert, what drives your pathetic need to express yourself through movement? Is it perhaps compensation for your complete lack of authentic artistic vision?"

"What do you mean?" Cohn asked, setting down Poopsy-Pops's carrier.

"I mean your so-called interpretive dance is nothing but bourgeois entertainment. Real art comes from genuine suffering, from confronting the darkness of existence. Not from whatever it is you do while wearing spandex."

"My art is meaningful," Cohn protested. "Just yesterday I performed 'The Anguish of Academic Pursuit' and—"

"Meaningless drivel!" Harvey interrupted. "The only suffering is by those watching your performance. And that condiment obsession of yours. Beige Poupon? Really? True artists don't mask the authentic flavor of food with artificial enhancements. Food should be consumed in its natural state, just as art should express raw, unfiltered emotion."

Cohn looked down at the jar of Beige Poupon he'd unconsciously pulled from his pocket. "But it enhances—"

"It corrupts! Just like your Ratty Rat obsession corrupts your ability to create genuine art. You're not an artist, Robert. You're a walking advertisement for the American consumer culture."

I could see Cohn's face starting to quiver. It reminded me again that ever since he'd met Brett, nothing had gone right for him. His dance performances were getting worse, he was losing at everything, and now even his fellow expatriates were turning on him.

"And that ridiculous animal," Harvey continued, gesturing toward Poopsy-Pops. "Carrying around someone else's pampered pet like a nursemaid. Where is your dignity, man?"

Before Cohn could answer, Frances appeared. But instead of her usual slightly frazzled appearance, she looked determined, almost fierce. She was walking directly toward our table with the purposeful stride of someone about to cause a scene.

"Uh-oh, here we go," I said.

"Robert Cohn!" Frances announced loudly as she reached our table. "We need to talk. Right here, right now."

"Frances, can't we discuss this privately—"

"No! I'm done with private discussions. I'm done with you entirely!"

A few people at nearby tables started to turn and watch. Frances seemed to notice and liked the audience.

"Ladies and gentlemen," she announced to the gathering crowd, "I'd like you to meet Robert Cohn, Princeton interpretive dance champion and full-time man-child!"

"Ooooh," said someone from a nearby table.

"Frances, please—"

"Please what? Please continue to pretend that you're a mature adult when you spend your days humming cartoon songs and carrying around my dog like a purse? Please keep pretending that your so-called 'art' isn't just an excuse to wear tight clothing and flail around embarrassingly?"

The crowd was growing. I could see people from inside Le Macabre coming out to watch.

"You want to know the truth about Robert?" Frances continued, her voice carrying across the café. "He's thirty-four years old and he's obsessed with Ratty Rat. Not just likes Ratty movies—obsessed. He sleeps with a Ratty Rat stuffed animal! He wants to visit a theme park that doesn't even exist yet!"

"Ahhhh," the crowd responded appreciatively.

"And the dancing! Oh, the dancing!" Frances was really hitting her stride now. "He calls it 'interpretive dance' but clearly whatever it is has no interpretation! Then he tells me that I don't understand art. Art? I can only describe it as a full body dry heave in tights!"

"You go, girl!" someone shouted from the crowd.

Cohn's face was getting redder and redder. Harvey was watching with obvious delight, sipping from one of his skull mugs.

"But the worst part," Frances announced, "is that he's not even a man. He's a child in a man's body who needs someone to take care of him, someone to make his decisions, someone to carry his condiments and walk his dog—well, my dog—and listen to him whine about cartoon characters! And all this time he would never marry me even though I've been so accepting of him."

The crowd was really into it now, applauding and cheering.

"So, I'm breaking up with you, Robert Cohn! Right here, in front of everyone, because you deserve to be publicly humiliated the same way you've been privately humiliating me for months!"

And then Robert Cohn, Princeton interpretive dance champion, started to cry. Not just tearing up—full-on sobbing, right there in front of Le Macabre.

"Awww," the crowd said, but not sympathetically.

"This is better than the vampire show," I heard someone whisper.

Frances looked at the crying Cohn and seemed to realize she wasn't finished. "You know what? You're pathetic!"

The crowd gasped. Cohn's sobbing got louder. Poopsy-Pops started whimpering in sympathy, which only made the whole scene more absurd.

"Frances," I said, clearing my throat loudly. "This is getting a bit—"

"Oh, Jake!" Frances turned to me with wild eyes. "Did you know he talks to his stuffed Ratty? Did you know that?"

The crowd erupted in laughter and applause.

I had enough of this awkwardness. It was time to go. "Harvey," I said loudly, "I just remembered I had a question about...uhmm, your vampireness."

Harvey, still in character, nodded solemnly. "Ah yes, my mystical power."

I stood up quickly, but as I glanced back, I saw Frances had apparently decided that verbal humiliation wasn't enough. She was now physically attacking Cohn, hitting him with her purse while the crowd cheered her on like it was a boxing match.

"Get him!" someone yelled.

"Hit him harder!" called another.

Harvey raised his skull mug in a toast. "To authentic human drama!"

I walked away quickly, leaving the sounds of applause, Frances's continued verbal assault, and Cohn's pathetic sobbing behind me. Poopsy-Pops was barking frantically, adding to the chaos.

As I made my way home, I reflected again on how Brett's curse seemed to be spreading. First Cohn lost his confidence, then his skills, and now his dignity was being beaten out of him by Frances in front of a cheering crowd at a vampire-themed café. I still wasn't sure how a curse could be possible. After all, this was Cohn we were talking about, and he had a habit of creating his own bad luck; but my senses were now awakened, and I resolved to be on the lookout for any new signs. I also resolved to find some new friends.

Chapter 7: The Count's Collapse and Brett's Vaca

I made good on my resolution and was having the best evening I'd had in months. Harvey Stone and a few new friends were over. Harvey was still in his gothic vampire persona. We had spread out a full Dungeons & Dragons campaign on my dining room table, complete with hand-drawn maps, painted miniature figures, and enough dice to supply a small casino.

"I cast a spell of eternal darkness upon the village," Harvey announced dramatically, rolling a twenty-sided die. His fake Transylvanian accent made everything sound more ominous.

"Excellent," said Marcus, an American painter who was surprisingly good at playing a dwarf warrior. "My character attacks the undead horde with his enchanted battle-axe."

"Wait," I said, consulting my notes as the dungeon master. "You have to roll for initiative first."

This was exactly what I needed. No Brett drama, no Cohn whining, no Frances beating anyone with purses. Just a group of grown men sitting around my table, drinking beer, and pretending to be wizards and warriors in an imaginary medieval world.

"Jake," Harvey said, dropping his accent temporarily, "this is the most authentic artistic expression I've experienced in months. The collaborative storytelling, the strategic thinking—it's far superior to interpretive dance."

"Yes, much better than watching Cohn flail around in a unitard," agreed Marcus.

We were just getting to the climactic battle scene when there was a loud knock at my door.

"Are you expecting anyone?" Harvey asked.

"No," I said, hoping whoever it was would go away.

The knocking persisted, followed by Brett's voice: "Jake! Darling! Let us in!"

My heart sank. I looked at the beautiful game setup, the intricate story we'd been building for hours, and the peaceful evening that was about to be destroyed.

"Jake!" Brett called again. "We know you're in there!"

I opened the door to find Brett and Count Cholesterol, who was somehow even larger than the last time I'd seen him. He was carrying what appeared to be several buckets of fried chicken, grease already seeping through the cardboard. The buckets of chicken had an image of his face and the logo of his restaurant chain: The Count's Heart-Stoppin' Chicken, with the famous slogan, "So Good, It'll Stop Your Heart!"

"Hello, darling," Brett said, pushing past me. "We brought dinner!"

Count Cholesterol wheezed his way through the door, immediately headed for the dining room table, and without any acknowledgment of what was already there, began setting down his greasy buckets directly on top of our carefully arranged game.

"No, wait—" I started.

But it was too late. Chicken grease was already seeping into our hand-drawn maps. The count's enormous bulk knocked over several painted miniatures as he arranged his feast. Our dice scattered across the floor.

"There we go," he panted, while rubbing his hands together. "The finest fried chicken in Paris. My own recipe."

Harvey, Marcus, and our other two players stared in horror as three hours of careful setup was destroyed in thirty seconds by cascading grease and chicken parts.

"Oh," Brett said, noticing the game for the first time. "Were you boys playing something?"

"We were," Harvey said icily, his gothic persona barely containing his rage, "creating collaborative art."

"How charming," Brett said, already heading for my liquor cabinet as she lit a cigarette. "Jake, what do you have here to drink?"

Marcus stood up slowly, wiping chicken grease off one of his miniature figures. "Well," he said, "I think I'll head home."

"Yes," Harvey agreed, gathering what remained of his dice. "The artistic mood has been—"

Up until now my friends had been staring at the ruined remnants of our game. As they began to look up, they caught a glimpse of Brett for the first time and, one by one, they froze and stared. Each of them started to move toward the exit but as Brett bent over to reach a bottle they seemed to lose all motor control.

Marcus walked directly into the doorframe, bounced off, and kept walking. Harvey tripped over his own cape while staring at Brett and had to grab the wall for support. Our friend Paul managed to collect all his things but then walked straight into the closed bathroom door, thinking it was the exit. And then there was Gerald, who was so mesmerized by Brett that he started backing toward the front door while staring at her.

He made his way through the door but then tumbled down the entire flight of stairs nearby. We could hear him bumping and rolling all the way to the bottom.

"Are you all right?" I called down.

"Fine!" came Gerald's voice from the lobby. "Totally fine! Beautiful evening!"

Within minutes, my apartment had gone from a peaceful gathering of friends to a grease-splattered disaster zone populated by one enormous count and one devastatingly attractive woman who had just destroyed my social life.

"Why did you even come over here?" I asked, surveying the ruins of our game.

"Oh, darling, we're so sorry," Brett said, not sounding sorry at all. "Aren't we sorry, count?"

The count was still breathing heavily from the stairs and seemed to be experiencing some kind of chest pain. "Very sorry, Mr. Barnes. Please, let me make it up to you."

He pulled out a wallet that was roughly the size of a phone book and began throwing money on the table. "For the games, for the inconvenience, for anything you need."

"You don't need to—"

"I insist!" More money appeared. "What about new games? Do you prefer Pokémon cards? Magic the Gathering? More of those little dragon figures?"

"It's fine," I said, though it clearly wasn't.

"Actually," Brett said, "we came over because the count needed to get out of the hospital. He's had quite a week."

I looked at Count Cholesterol, who was now leaning heavily against my wall and sweating profusely.

"Twenty heart attacks in the last three days," Brett explained cheerfully, as if this was perfectly normal. "The doctors think all the grease in his system is actually helping now. His arteries are completely lubricated."

As she said this, the count clutched his chest and made a small groaning sound.

"Another one?" Brett asked.

"Small one," he wheezed. "I'm fine."

"The doctors say as long as they're under five minutes, he should be okay."

I stared at them. "You came to my apartment because he's having multiple daily heart attacks?"

"Oh, it's not just that," Brett said, flicking ash from her cigarette onto my rug. "We want to take you out for dinner and dancing!"

I stared at this man who was literally dying in front of me, and the woman who had just destroyed my peaceful evening and scared away all my friends, and who was now suggesting we go out and pretend this was all normal.

"Why me?" I asked. "Why is it always me?"

"Because you're such a good *friend*, darling," Brett said, grinding her cigarette into my rug.

Just then, a telegram boy appeared at my door. Count Cholesterol signed for it, read it, and his face went white.

"What is it?" Brett asked.

"My chicken farm near Detroit," he said weakly. "Completely bankrupt. Something about a salmonella outbreak."

"Well," Brett said brightly, "more reason to celebrate! Let's go to dinner!"

I looked around my ruined apartment, thought about my scattered friends, and realized I had a choice. I could send them away and spend the evening cleaning chicken grease off my belongings, or I could go out with them and at least get a free meal before Count Cholesterol's inevitable complete financial collapse.

Also, I was hungry, and the chicken smelled pretty good. Although, I wasn't sure why we were going out since he brought chicken but since he was paying, I didn't question it.

"Fine," I said. "Let's go."

We went to the fanciest restaurant in Paris, "The Golden Chicken," which seemed appropriate given the count's business interests. The irony was not lost on anyone when we arrived and the count immediately ordered more fried chicken.

During dinner, Count Cholesterol had two more heart attacks but seemed to recover each time by eating more chicken. A telegram arrived informing him that another of his businesses had failed. Then another telegram about his chain of truck stops going into bankruptcy.

"My goodness," Brett said, "you're having quite a run of bad luck."

"It's strange," the count said, clutching his chest again. "Everything was fine until—" He looked at Brett and seemed to realize something but didn't finish the sentence.

"You know," he said between bites of chicken, "you two make a lovely couple. Why aren't you together?"

"Oh, I'm engaged to Mike Campbell," Brett said casually.

The count nearly choked on his chicken. "Engaged? But I thought—how many men are you involved with exactly?"

"Well," Brett said, counting on her fingers, "there's Mike, and Jake's my dear friend, and you're my new friend, and there are a few others here and there. *Technically*, I'm still married right now too."

"Wow, I appreciate the whole 'liberated woman' thing you have going but maybe you should set some kind of criteria," the count said, looking simultaneously impressed and terrified.

"Oh, I do," Brett said cheerfully while patting his wallet.

After dinner, we went dancing. Count Cholesterol couldn't actually dance due to his size and medical condition, so he sat at a table eating more chicken while Brett and I danced. She seemed perfectly happy, laughing and enjoying herself.

Then, suddenly, as we were dancing, her mood changed completely.

"Oh, darling," she said, "I'm so miserable."

Here we go again, I thought. *Here we go again.*

"You were happy five minutes ago," I said.

"I know, but now I'm just terribly sad. I think it's because the Count's businesses keep failing. It's rather putting a damper on things."

So that was it. The money was running out, and Brett was already losing interest.

"I think I want to go home," she said.

"Of course you do."

"Will you be a good friend and take me home?"

A good friend. There it was again.

"Sure," I said.

We said farewell to Count Cholesterol, who had received three more telegrams about failing businesses and was looking rather pale despite his continued chicken consumption.

I took Brett back to her hotel. At the door, she turned to me with a bright smile.

"Thanks, darling. You're such a wonderful friend. You might not see me for a while as I am going to San Sebastian for a little vaca," she said.

A little Vaca? Her whole life was a vacation. Immediately I thought she must have found someone new to drain the life out of.

"Are you going with anyone special?" I asked.

"Oh, definitely not. Nope, just me. You know how much I like the quiet. It should be good for me to get away and drink some water for once."

Yep, she was definitely lying.

She held up her hand for a high-five.

I stared at her hand for a moment, then gave her the most pathetic high-five in the history of human interaction.

"Good night, Brett."

"Good night, Jake!"

She walked into her hotel, leaving me standing on the street corner, wondering how my pleasant evening of fantasy gaming had turned into escorting a woman through another man's financial and cardiac collapse.

The Brett curse was getting stronger, and apparently, I was just going along for the ride.

Book II: The Tab Rises

Chapter 8: A Pokémon Champ and a Beer Hat

I did not see Brett again until she came back from San Sebastian, and honestly, it was the most peaceful month I'd had in years. Without Brett's chaos and Cohn's obsessiveness, I'd managed to return to semi-normal human activities. I'd had weekly card nights with friends, gone bowling, seen some movies, and even found some rare Pokémon cards at a local shop. For the first time in months, I wasn't dealing with interpretive dance emergencies or women complaining about only meeting five millionaires per week.

One letter did come from her from San Sebastian. It had a picture of the beach and said: "Darling, having a marvelous time drinking lots of water and definitely not here with anyone special. Definitely alone. Love to all the chaps. Brett."

The suspicious thing was that the stationery was from "Studio Expresión," which I remembered because Cohn had mentioned how much he'd liked that particular dance studio when he'd visited Spain. He'd gone on about how they "truly understood his artistic vision" and "respected his interpretative work." This seemed like an odd coincidence, but then again, maybe Brett had just picked up random stationery.

Still, I couldn't shake the feeling that she wasn't alone. That's what Brett does—she drains the life from men like some kind of beautiful vampire. Harvey Stone might play at being one, but Brett was the real thing.

For a moment, I found myself thinking that maybe Cohn should date Brett. If the curse worked on him too, it would solve everyone's problems. Although the thought of those two together was so disgusting that I immediately pushed it out of my mind. That would be one of the worst things that could possibly happen.

My friend, Bill Gorton, was scheduled to arrive at the end of June, and we were planning to leave for Spain for a fishing trip—well, technically a visit to a "trout farm" where they guaranteed you'd catch fish. It was basically fishing for people who didn't know how to fish, but it sounded relaxing enough. After the fishing trip we planned to go to the Fiesta and the Running of the Roosters in Pamplona, Spain.

He was a professional Pokémon card player and had been away at a tournament. Yes, you read that correctly. In a story already featuring interpretive dance championships and Ratty Rat obsessions, somehow professional Pokémon playing seems like the most reasonable career choice anyone's made so far.

When Bill finally arrived, I heard his taxi stop and went to the window and called to him. He waved and started up the stairs carrying his bags and what appeared to be several Pokémon card binders.

"Well," I said, "how was your trip?"

"Wonderful," he said. "I think. I think I won something. I have all these trophies."

"I thought I read that you won the championship?"

"I mean, I won, but I don't remember how."

"How do you mean?"

"Drunk, Jake. I was drunk the entire tournament."

"On that note, let's go get you a drink. Maybe that will jog your memory."

We walked over to the nearest café and ordered a few drinks because it didn't matter what time of the day it was, this is what we do in this book.

Bill rubbed his forehead. "Remarkable thing," he said. "Don't know how it happened. Suddenly I was the champion."

"You were drunk the entire time?"

"Four days, Jake. The entire tournament."

"What Pokémon did you use?"

"Don't remember. But apparently I had a Charizard. Found this trophy that says, 'First Place - Advanced Charizard Division.'"

"Do anything else?"

"Not so sure. Possible."

"Take that drink and remember."

"Might remember a little," Bill said after taking a long drink. "I remember something about a final battle. Enormous crowd. Had a kid opponent, couldn't have been more than twelve. Remember the kid perfectly."

"Go on."

"Sweet kid. Very serious about his Pokémon strategy. All of a sudden I apparently played some card that made everyone cheer. Not sure what I did. Kid started crying. Felt terrible about it."

"Then what happened?"

"Gave the kid some of my prize money and went around with him to buy more cards. Turned into a whole thing. Think I might have started a Pokémon charity for sad children."

"Sounds like you had a good time."

"Must have," Bill said as he finished his drink.

We went outside. Bill was still carrying his Pokémon binders and seemed to be having trouble walking straight.

"Where should we go?"

"Want to eat somewhere?"

"Sure."

As we walked down the Boulevard, we ran into Harvey Stone near his usual gothic café. He was still dressed entirely in black and looked like he hadn't seen sunlight since our D&D game.

"Ah, Jacob," Harvey said in his fake accent. "And who is this Pokémon master?"

"This is Bill Gorton. Bill, Harvey Stone."

"Charmed," Harvey said dramatically. "I sense you are also an appreciator of games of strategy and chance."

"Love 'em," Bill said, brightening up. "Got any good card games going?"

"Indeed. We were just discussing the philosophical implications of different gaming systems. Pokémon versus Magic: The Gathering versus traditional—"

HONK! HONK! HONK!

A taxi had pulled up right next to us, honking loudly. Through the window, I could see Brett waving frantically.

Oh, for Pete's sake, I thought.

"What is with this woman haunting me?" I said to no one in particular.

Brett got out of the taxi. Bill took one look at her and his entire demeanor changed.

"Wow! Pretty Laaadeeeeyyy!" he said in what I can only describe as a weird Jerry Lewis voice.

Harvey just stood there, staring at Brett with the intensity of someone who had actually seen a vampire.

"Hullo!" Brett said. "Hullo! I'm just back from San Sebastian. I drank so much water there I need a proper drink immediately or I might die."

"This is Bill Gorton. Lady Ashley," I said.

Brett smiled at Bill, who was still staring at her with his mouth hanging open.

"I must get a drink," Brett said. "Absolutely must."

"We just had a few drinks and we were going to get something to eat," I said. "What do you think Bill, do you want to eat or get a drink with Brett?"

He just stood shaking his head yes while staring at Brett. Brett and I agreed that this meant he needed another drink. I mean, who needs to eat when you're an expatriate in Paris?

We left Harvey standing there, still staring after Brett like she'd cast some kind of spell on him.

At the nearest café, Brett immediately ordered a whiskey and soda.

"How was San Sebastian?" I asked.

"Oh, marvelous," Brett said, already halfway through her first drink. "I'm a completely new person. All I did was exercise, eat right, and meditate. Very spiritual. Very pure. And I'm going to stay that way."

She finished her drink and immediately ordered another.

"Didn't drink at all?" Bill asked, still staring at her.

"Not a drop," Brett said, starting on her second whiskey. "Well, maybe a little wine with meals. And possibly some champagne in the evenings. And I think there might have been some brandy for medicinal purposes. But other than that, completely sober."

She was already signaling for a third drink.

"She's amazing," Bill whispered to me.

"She's engaged," I said. *"And cursed."* I whispered the last part and Bill gave me a strange look.

"I have to get going," Brett said, standing up after finishing her third drink in ten minutes. "Mike's coming in tonight. You simply must meet him. Come to Café Reject around ten."

"We'll be there," I said, though I had no idea why I kept agreeing to these things.

That evening, we made our way to Café Reject, where the sign still proudly declared "Rejecting Reality One Drink at a Time." Inside, we found Mike Campbell at a corner table. Mike was wearing what appeared to be a beer hat—one of those contraptions with drink holders on each side and straws that came down to your mouth. He also had three separate drinks arranged in front of him on the table. When he saw us approaching, he stood up unsteadily.

"Hel-lo, Jake!" he said. "Hel-lo! Hel-lo! How are you, old lad?"

"You look very… hydrated, Mike."

"Oh, I am. I'm frightfully hydrated. I've done nothing but drink. Drink all day long."

"Mike, this is Bill Gorton."

"Pleasure!" Mike said, swaying slightly. "I say, have you seen my Brett? Isn't she beautiful? She's the most beautiful woman in Paris. More beautiful than anyone else's girlfriend!"

"She's quite attractive," Bill said diplomatically.

"Attractive? ATTRACTIVE?" Mike was getting louder. "She's a goddess! She's coming home with me tonight! She'll never leave me! I'm the best! She's with ME! She's hotter than any of your girlfriends, isn't she?"

Brett appeared from the bar, looking slightly embarrassed.

"Michael, dear, perhaps tone it down a bit?"

"Brett! There she is! My beautiful Brett! Isn't she gorgeous? Look at her! She chose ME!"

Brett looked at us apologetically. "He's been like this since he got off the train."

"I'm only a little drunk," Mike announced to the entire café. "Just a tiny bit! Brett, tell them how beautiful you are!"

"This is going to be a long evening," I muttered to Bill.

"I heard there's a great mini golf course around here," Bill said. "Want to go tomorrow?"

"Of course," I said. Bill and I proceeded to discuss our plans for the next day. Anything to get away from Mike's beer hat and his public declarations of ownership over Brett.

As the evening progressed, Mike continued his performance, alternately declaring Brett's beauty to anyone who would listen and challenging random men to admit she was more attractive than their companions. Brett, meanwhile, worked her way through several more drinks.

I found myself watching them and thinking about the Brett curse. Mike seemed happy now, but I wondered how long it would take for his luck to turn. Given his current trajectory, I suspected it wouldn't be long.

After a while Bill and I could take no more and left for the night.

"I'll see you tomorrow for mini golf," I told Bill.

I was hoping we could have at least one normal, drama-free day before leaving for Spain. Plus, who doesn't like mini golf?

Chapter 9: Unwanted Guests and Torn ACLs

The mini golf course in Paris is without a doubt the best mini golf course in the world. Bill and I played the best rounds we could remember. Our favorite hole had to be the croissant-themed one where you had to putt through a giant buttery pastry.

Back at my flat, I found a letter waiting for me from Cohn, which was strange because Cohn usually didn't write letters. The envelope was thick and expensive looking.

"Dear Jake," it read, "I am having a wonderful time here in Hendaye. I have been excelling at everything—golf, bridge, swimming, even some local dance competitions. The people here truly appreciate authentic artistic expression. I miss my friends terribly and am very much looking forward to our fishing trip. By the way, how is Lady Brett? I hope she is well. Your friend, Robert."

I stared at the letter. Something was off. First, when had Cohn been invited fishing with us? Second, Cohn never talked about "excelling" at things unless he was trying to impress someone. Third, he'd asked about Brett in a way that seemed calculated to sound casual. And fourth—I looked at the stationery more closely—it was the exact same letterhead as Brett's postcard from San Sebastian. "Studio Expresión" was printed at the top.

My stomach dropped. It couldn't be true. Could it? Had Brett actually gone to Spain with Robert Cohn? The most annoying person in all of Europe? The man who hummed Ratty Rat songs while spreading Beige Poupon on ice cream?

I wrote back quickly, telling him he could join us at the trout farm and giving him instructions on where to meet us. But my peaceful fishing trip was already feeling doomed.

That evening, I stopped by the Dingo to clear my head. The Dingo was an Australian-themed bar, complete with koala mugs and drinks served in hollowed-out boomerangs. I'd never been sure why someone had decided Paris needed an Australian-themed establishment, but the drinks were strong and that's all that mattered tonight.

Of course, Brett and Mike were sitting at the bar.

I stood there for a moment, contemplating the cosmic joke that was my life. I could have gone to any bar in Paris—I could have gone to a bar in Morocco—and somehow these two would have been there waiting for me. It was like being trapped in a nightmare designed specifically to test my sanity.

Mike still had his beer hat on, though it was now askew and one of the straws was bent.

"Hello, darling," Brett said. "Just the person I wanted to see."

"Hello, Jake," Mike said. "I say, I understand you're going down to Spain. To that festival thing—Pamplona?"

"Yes, Bill and I are going fishing first, then—"

"Splendid! We'd love to come along, wouldn't we, Brett? You wouldn't mind if we joined you?"

My heart sank. "Well, I—"

"It would be grand," Mike continued, not waiting for my answer and patting me hard on the back. "Brett's mad to go. You wouldn't mind, would you? We wouldn't be a bloody nuisance."

I looked at their expectant faces and felt my peaceful trip slipping away. "Of course not," I heard myself saying.

"Brilliant!" Mike stood up unsteadily. "I'm going to the barber's to get ready for the trip. Must look my best for Spain!"

He wandered off, leaving his beer hat on the bar.

Brett and I sat in silence for a moment.

"Jake," she said finally, "there's something I need to tell you."

"What?"

"About San Sebastian. I wasn't exactly alone."

"I know," I said. "You were with Robert Cohn."

Brett looked surprised. "How did you—"

"The stationery. You both used the same letterhead."

"Oh." She took a long drink. "Well, yes. I was with Robert."

I felt the room spin slightly. For a moment, everything went black, and I had to grip the bar to steady myself.

"Jake? Are you all right?"

"I'm fine," I said, though I wasn't. "I just… why? Why him?"

"What do you mean?"

"Brett, you won't date me because of my toe fungus, but you'll go away with a man who does interpretive dance and obsesses over Ratty Rat? The dancing, the Beige Poupon, the Cohn-ness of it all. How could you?"

Brett looked down at her drink. "Well, you see, I found out his family has quite a lot of money. More than I initially thought. Much more."

"So, it was about money."

"It's always about money, darling. But honestly, I couldn't handle him for very long. Do you know he tried to perform an interpretive dance about our 'romantic connection' on the beach? In front of other people? And he kept asking if I wanted to plan our future trip to Rattyland."

"You broke it off?"

"Had to. It was either that or throw myself off a cliff. But Jake, do you think he'll be all right about it? Coming on this trip?"

I stared at her. "Do you think *I'll* be all right about it? You've just told me you had an affair with the most annoying man in Europe, and now you want to bring him and your drunken fiancé on my trip I've planned all year. Did anyone ask if *I'd* be okay with all this drama being loaded up as unnecessary baggage?"

"Don't be dramatic, darling."

"I'm being dramatic? I planned a simple trip with Bill to a trout farm where they guaranteed you'd catch fish. Then we were going to go to the festival at Pamplona. Now it's turning into a traveling circus with you, Mike, Cohn, and Cohn's big fat head."

"It'll be fun," Brett said unconvincingly.

Three days later, Bill and I took the train to Bayonne. The ride was uneventful, which I thought would be the last peace

I'd have for a while. Before we left, I gave Brett and Mike travel instructions and an itinerary.

When we got off at the station, we saw Cohn waiting for us. He looked out of sorts and didn't even notice that we had arrived. He was wearing a brown fur coat. Underneath that he had on an ultra-tight shirt that read 'Dance Revolution' and topped it all off with one of those tiny Ratty Rat backpacks. He was holding a café latte, a drink he claimed to have invented.

But something was clearly wrong with him. He had dark circles under his eyes and he was clearly muttering a word or phrase continually. He was standing awkwardly, favoring one leg, and he looked nervous.

As we got closer all I heard was, "Brett…Brett…Brett."

Bill turned to me and said, "You've got to be kidding me. This is the guy coming with us to fish? Are you sure you're friends with this guy?"

"Not so sure anymore," I said while shaking my head. We both started laughing.

We walked up to Cohn and I had to literally tap him on the shoulder to snap him out of this daze he was in. It was then that I saw he was wearing a bracelet that read, 'Brett', and had hearts on both sides of the name.

"Hello, Jake," he said, trying to smile. "Have a good trip?"

"Fine," I said. "This is Bill Gorton."

"How are you?" Bill said, shaking Cohn's hand.

"Robert, are you limping?" I asked.

"Oh, this?" Cohn gestured vaguely at his leg. "I hurt my knee in Spain. Possibly tore my ACL. It was very strange—I was perfectly fine, and then suddenly during a dance performance, my knee just gave out completely."

The Brett curse strikes again, I thought.

"Come on," Cohn said, "I've got a cab."

As we got into the taxi, Bill leaned over and whispered to me, "Wow, you were right. This guy is weird. How did you get mixed up with all these people?"

"Long story," I muttered.

"Are you sure you still want to go through with this trip?"

I looked at Cohn, who was nervously fidgeting with his bracelet and wincing every time the cab hit a bump. I could still hear him muttering under his breath.

"We could just leave," Bill whispered. "Not tell anyone. Just disappear."

For a moment, I seriously considered it. We could get back on the train, go somewhere else, anywhere else. But we already had reservations, and somehow I knew that even if we tried to escape, this group would find a way to track us down.

"No," I said resignedly. "Let's just get it over with."

As we drove through the dark streets of Bayonne, I realized that my peaceful fishing trip had officially become a disaster before it had even begun.

We stopped at the hotel room and Cohn requested help with his luggage and backpack. Even though everything else was falling apart, the hotel was nice. We each had our own room and they had free Continental Breakfast in the morning so at least I had that going for me.

Chapter 10: Cohn's Secret and Broken Friendships

In the morning we went down for the hotel's "free Continental breakfast," which turned out to be stale rolls, questionable cheese, and what appeared to be jam that had developed its own ecosystem. The dining room was crawling with roaches the size of small dogs, and flies circled overhead like tiny vultures. The staff seemed completely unbothered by this, stepping over cockroaches while serving coffee that looked like it had been filtered through dirty socks.

"I think I'll stick to beer for breakfast," Bill said, watching a roach drag away half a croissant.

"Good idea," I agreed. "At least beer is probably sterile. Plus, you get *some* nutrition from it, right?"

Cohn appeared wearing the same fur coat and was carrying a fresh new café latte in one hand and a bottle of Beige Poupon in the other.

"I see you gentlemen are having the continental breakfast," he said, sipping his drink. "I had them make me a latte. You know, I invented this drink while I was in San Sebastian. I call it a 'latte.' It's espresso with steamed milk. I think it might catch on."

Bill and I stared at him. "Robert, lattes have existed for—"

"No, no," Cohn interrupted. "This is my invention, all me."

After choking down what we could of breakfast, we went to arrange transportation to Pamplona. Cohn insisted he could handle the negotiations since he claimed to speak Spanish.

"Yo quiero uno automobile por Pamplona," he announced to the man at the garage.

The man looked confused and responded in rapid Spanish.

"Sí, sí," Cohn nodded confidently. "Muy bueno. Gracias."

The man led us out to what appeared to be a golf cart.

"Perfect!" Cohn announced. "I knew my Spanish would come in handy."

Bill and I looked at the golf cart, which had a maximum speed of approximately fifteen miles per hour and no roof.

"Robert," I said, "this is a golf cart."

"It's exactly what I ordered. A small automobile for recreational purposes."

Bill and I exchanged glances and quickly went back to speak with the garage owner ourselves. After some actual communication, we arranged for a proper car.

The drive through the Spanish countryside would have been the most beautiful thing I'd ever seen if it hadn't been for Cohn. Rolling green hills, ancient forests, crystal-clear streams, and spectacular waterfalls cascaded down mountainsides. The landscape was breathtaking.

Unfortunately, Cohn had fallen asleep immediately after getting in the car and was now snoring loudly, drooling on his fur coat, and occasionally making strange humming sounds in his sleep. Every few minutes he would shift position and his injured knee would bump against something, causing him to let out little yelps without waking up.

"Look at that waterfall," Bill whispered, pointing to a magnificent cascade.

"Incredible," I whispered back, not wanting to wake Cohn.

"And those mountains—"

"SNORE! R-A-T-T-Y... SNORE!" Cohn interrupted our appreciation of nature's beauty.

Bill shook his head. "This guy could ruin a sunset."

We finally arrived at the Hotel Hen House in Pamplona. Montoya, the hotel's owner and old friend greeted me warmly.

"Jake! Welcome back! This year's rooster fighting season is going to be spectacular. The birds are more vicious than ever, and their beaks have been sharpened to razor perfection. I hear there might even be a new breed of rooster used this year, the Supreme Rooster."

"Wonderful," I said. "Any promising new fighters this year?"

"Ah, yes! There's a young man, Pedro Romero. Only nineteen, but he has natural talent with the roosters. I want to keep him away from the tourists and corrupting influences, you understand? He must remain pure for the art of rooster fighting."

"Of course. I respect that."

"You are a true aficionado, Jake. Not like these other tourists who come just for the spectacle."

We got our rooms and went down for lunch. The dining room was blissfully free of insects, and the food was excellent. Cohn, who had somehow managed to injure his other leg getting out of the car, was limping more dramatically than ever.

"Well," I said during the meal, "Brett and Mike should be in tonight."

"I don't think they'll come," Cohn said confidently.

"Why not?" Bill asked.

"I know they won't come tonight," Cohn repeated, with that superior air that made everyone want to hit him.

"I'll bet you fifty pesetas they're here tonight," Bill said.

"Make it a hundred," Cohn smiled smugly. "I know they won't be here."

After lunch, Cohn announced he was going for a "full spa treatment."

"I need a facial, massage, manicure, pedicure, and hair styling," he said. "I want to look my absolute best."

"For what?" I asked. "I thought you said they weren't coming."

"Just… in case," he said, and limped off to find a spa.

That evening, as we were sitting at Café Loco, I checked my watch. "Train should be here soon. We should head to the station."

Cohn appeared, looking like he'd been through a beauty salon hurricane. His face was glowing from some kind of treatment, his hair was slicked back with what appeared to be an entire jar of pomade, and he smelled like he'd fallen into a vat of cologne.

"Ready!" he announced.

"I thought you said they weren't coming," Bill said.

"They're not. But if they do come, I'll be ready."

Cohn and I left for the station. Bill said he didn't want to leave his dinner, but I knew the real reason was that he didn't want to be around Cohn. At the station, the train arrived and passengers disembarked, but no Brett and Mike. Cohn's confidence seemed to deflate with each person who wasn't them.

Back at the hotel, we found Bill setting up a game of Uno in the bar.

"How'd it go?" he asked.

"They didn't come," I said.

Just then, Montoya approached with a telegram. "This came for you."

I opened it. It read:

"Still in San Sebastian but on our way. -Brett"

I looked at Cohn, who was sitting there looking dejected despite his perfect spa treatment, and felt a sudden urge to torture him.

"It's from Brett," I announced. "It says, 'Cohn, I still love you.'"

Cohn's eyes went wide. "Really? She said that?"

"Read it yourself."

But before I could hand him the telegram, Cohn jumped up excitedly, shouting "YES!" Unfortunately, his injured knee gave out, causing him to fall sideways and smash his head against the corner of the table. Blood immediately began streaming down his face, and he knocked over everyone's drinks in the process.

"I KNEW IT!" he yelled, struggling to stay conscious while blood dripped onto his fur coat. "I knew she loved me!"

"Cohn, you're bleeding everywhere," Bill said.

"She loves me and she'll love me forever!" Cohn continued, swaying unsteadily. "I love her more than anything! I'm better than you, Jake, because she chose to stay with me! That's right! Take your little toe problem and get out of here! She wants a dance champion, not a fungus failure!"

That was it. I'd had enough.

"Robert," I said, standing up, "if you love her so much, you better stay here and wait for her. Bill and I are leaving for fishing tomorrow."

"What?"

"You heard me. Plus, with that head wound and your aggravated knee injury, you better just stay here and get medical attention."

Bill was nodding enthusiastically. "That's an amazing idea, Jake. This guy makes me sick. The best thing that could happen is if he doesn't come fishing with us." He said this right in front of Cohn. You can see how Bill is a real friend.

"But... but..." Cohn was holding a napkin to his bleeding head, trying to focus his eyes.

"Who needs Cohn?" Bill continued. "Who needs Brett? You know what we need? New friends. Normal friends who don't bleed on furniture or drool in fur coats."

"I don't drool!" Cohn protested weakly.

"You do," I said. "You drool, you snore, you make Ratty Rat sounds in your sleep, and you think you invented lattes. Stay here and wait for your beloved Brett."

Cohn looked like he was about to cry, which would have been the perfect ending to this disaster of an evening.

"Come on, Bill," I said. "Let's go pack for our fishing trip."

As we left the bar, I could hear Cohn calling after us: "She really said she loves me, right? Right? The telegram really said that?"

"Sure, Robert," I called back. "Whatever helps you sleep at night."

Tomorrow, Bill and I would continue on our peaceful fishing trip in Burguete. Just the two of us, some trout, and zero Cohn.

Chapter 11: Circus Performers and Drinks Included

It was baking hot in the square when we came out after lunch, carrying our bags and the rod-case to go to Burguete. Last night we found there was only one available bus to Burguete. What we didn't know was it just happened to be the bus of the local circus troupe, Circe De Sowhat. The bus was already crowded when we approached. Performers were performing acrobatic stunts on top of the bus—some were doing handstands, others were building a human pyramid, and one man was literally doing flying somersaults from the roof to the ground and back up again.

Bill and I were about to climb up onto the bus when we heard a strange creaking sound. We turned around to see Robert Cohn. He was sitting in an old wooden wheelchair with a blanket over his lap, looking like someone's decrepit grandfather. His head was still bandaged from last night's incident, and both his legs were now wrapped in what appeared to be medical tape.

Bill did a double take. "Are you ok there, big guy?" he said.

"Oh, I'm fine," he said clutching what looked to be an empty bottle of Beige Poupon. "I found a way that if my legs give out I can still achieve artistic perfection."

"Hey!" he called out to the circus performers. "Check this out!"

He began doing some bizarre hand routine, wiggling his fingers and making flowing gestures while sitting in his wheelchair. The circus performers stopped their acrobatics and stared at him in fascination.

"Is this typical for Americans?" one of them asked me in a thick Spanish accent.

"No," I said. "This isn't typical for humans in general."

The performers weren't sure what to think. Within minutes, they had formed their own human wheelchair—some of them got on their hands and knees to be the wheels, while others formed the seat and back. They then proceeded to wheel around the square, limping and making exaggerated groaning sounds while doing Cohn's ridiculous hand dance.

Cohn watched this mockery of himself and somehow took it as appreciation. "See? They understand my art!"

"It's ok, Robert," I said. "You just rest up here and we'll meet up with you later."

Bill and I climbed aboard the bus, shaking our heads. The bus finally started, and Cohn waved goodbye to us from his wheelchair. All the circus performers waved back while still cracking jokes about him.

As we headed out of town, we entered a tunnel. I heard a loud THUNK from above, followed by someone yelling. One of the acrobats who had been standing on the roof had been knocked off by the tunnel entrance.

"Does that happen often?" I asked.

"All the time," said one performer casually. "We lose about one person per trip. He'll catch up at the next stop."

As we were making small talk with some of the performers I took a drink from my wineskin. I noticed one of the performers looking at me with a sly smile on his face. A few miles down the road, he pulled out a wineskin and announced, "Americans! You must learn to drink properly!"

He grabbed the wineskin and proceeded to drain the entire contents in one continuous gulp, like some kind of professional drinking competitor. When he finished, he crushed the empty wineskin in his hand as if it were an aluminum can and let out a tremendous roar.

"Now you try!" he said to Bill.

But before Bill could even attempt it, wine tubes began appearing from various compartments throughout the bus. Apparently, this vehicle had been modified with a complete beverage distribution system. Wine was flowing to every seat through little tubes, like some kind of mobile bar.

"This is normal?" I asked.

"Of course! How else would you travel?" One of the acrobats said.

The wine flowed freely as we drove through the beautiful Spanish countryside. The performers continued their stunts while drinking—one man was doing backflips while sipping wine through a tube, another was juggling while simultaneously drinking from three different wine skins.

After about an hour, the bus stopped.

"Bathroom break!" the driver announced.

Everyone piled off the bus. The performers relieved themselves while continuing to drink and do handstands. After ten minutes, we piled back on.

Twenty minutes later, we stopped again.

"What's this stop for?" Bill asked.

"We always stop at this bar," the driver announced cheerfully. "It helps us fulfill our requirement."

"Requirement?"

"For this book. Don't you know every chapter must have drinking? It's how we deepen the plot philosophically."

We stopped at a small posada where the performers immediately began a drinking contest with the locals. Wine, beer, and various liqueurs flowed freely. I lost count of how many different beverages were consumed.

Back on the bus, we continued through increasingly mountainous terrain. As we climbed higher, it got noticeably colder. The circus performers began putting on layers of clothing while continuing their acrobatics, which was quite a sight.

"It's getting cold up here," Bill said.

"It's high," I said. "Must be twelve hundred meters."

"It's awful cold," Bill agreed.

When we finally arrived in Burguete, the driver stopped the bus and we got off. That's when we realized that three performers were still on the roof, and they appeared to be frozen solid in various acrobatic positions.

"Should we help them?" I asked.

"They'll thaw out eventually," said one of their companions. "Happens every time."

We collected our bags and walked through the small town to the inn. The woman who ran the place came out from the kitchen and shook hands with us.

"You need rooms?" she asked in Spanish.

"Yes," I said. "How much?"

She looked us up and down, clearly sizing us up as tourists. "Twenty pesetas per person."

"That seems expensive."

"Includes all drinks," she said quickly.

"All drinks?"

"Yes, yes. Wine, beer, liqueur, anything you want. All included."

Bill and I exchanged glances. "Do you drink a lot?" she asked nervously.

"Us? No, hardly at all," I said with a straight face. "Maybe a glass of wine with dinner."

"Very little drinking," Bill agreed. "We're practically teetotalers."

She looked relieved. "Good, good. Then twenty pesetas is fine."

"Deal," I said.

She showed us to our room, which was freezing cold. The wind was howling outside, rattling the shutters. There were two beds, a washstand, and a big steel engraving of some historical figure on the wall.

"This cold and for twenty pesetas!" Bill said. "I can see my breath."

We put on sweaters and went downstairs to the dining room, which had a stone floor and low ceiling. It was so cold that no matter where we were our breath steamed in the air.

"I need to warm up," Bill said, as he got up and started doing some jumping jacks.

I went to find the innkeeper. "Could we get some drinks to warm up?"

"Of course! All included!"

Within minutes, she brought out brandy, rum, wine, and hot punches. We started drinking steadily to combat the cold.

"More brandy?" she asked after we'd finished the first bottle.

"All included, right?" Bill said.

Her smile became a bit strained. "Yes… all included."

By dinnertime, we even impressed ourselves by how much we drank and were feeling quite warm despite the freezing temperatures. The innkeeper kept bringing out more bottles, though her expression grew increasingly concerned with each empty bottle we handed back.

"You said you hardly drink," she said nervously as she brought out the sixth bottle of wine.

"This is hardly drinking," I said. "For us, this is practically abstinence."

"We're just getting started," Bill added cheerfully. "This is actually how we hydrate ourselves."

After dinner, we continued drinking in our room to stay warm. The innkeeper came up twice to check on us, and each time we requested more beverages.

"All included, right?" Bill would say.

"Yes," she would reply weakly, "all included."

By the end of the evening, I counted at least fifteen empty bottles scattered around our room. The innkeeper looked like she was calculating whether she'd need to declare bankruptcy.

But you know what? Despite the freezing cold I was amazed at how much fun we were already having.

"This is great," Bill said, raising his glass. "No Ratty Rat songs, no Beige Poupon, and unlimited drinks."

"And no drama," I added.

We drank a toast to our freedom from annoying people and then got ready for bed. As I drifted off to sleep in our freezing room, warmed only by an impressive amount of alcohol, I had no idea that our peaceful fishing expedition would soon take us to the most ridiculous place on earth. Sometimes God has a sense of humor about these things.

Chapter 12: Trout Land and the Curse Expanded

When I woke in the morning I went to the window and looked out. The weather had cleared and there were no clouds on the mountains. The early morning was absolutely perfect—peaceful and beautiful in a way that made me remember why I'd wanted to get away from all the chaos in the first place.

Outside under the window, some goats were grazing peacefully. A family of deer had wandered down from the hills and were drinking from a small stream. Rabbits hopped around without a care in the world, and birds were singing in the trees. Then the animals simultaneously turned toward my window and looked up at me; they seemed to be singing directly to me. I nodded at one of the rabbits—he nodded back. Everything was in perfect harmony. The sunrise painted the mountains in brilliant colors, and for the first time in months, I felt completely at peace.

Bill was still sleeping, so I dressed quietly and went downstairs. The innkeeper was already up, looking significantly less worried about bankruptcy than she had the night before. Apparently, she'd decided to charge the circus performers triple rates to make up for our alcohol consumption.

"Good morning!" she said cheerfully. "How are you up after all of that drinking?"

"Well, it's a book so there are no real consequences. After all, in the original no one even seemed to get sick and that was supposedly based on actual events."

"Coffee?"

"That would be wonderful."

I sat outside with my coffee, watching the peaceful scene and thinking about how good it felt to be away from everything.

After a while, I went back upstairs to wake Bill.

"Come on," I said. "Time to get up."

"What? Get up? I never get up," he mumbled from under the covers.

"We're going fishing at the trout farm."

"Fishing? Why didn't you say fishing? I thought you just wanted me to get up for fun. Fishing? Fine. Now you're reasonable."

We had an excellent breakfast—the innkeeper had apparently decided to feed us well in hopes we wouldn't drink her completely out of business—and then packed our gear for the day's adventure.

The walk through the countryside was exactly what I'd needed. Rolling hills, ancient forests, crystal-clear streams, and that perfect mountain air that made you feel like you could walk forever. Bill and I barely talked, just enjoying the peace and the beautiful landscape.

"This is perfect," Bill said as we walked along a path through a grove of huge trees.

"Beyond perfect," I agreed.

It was so silent in this part of the woods that sticks broken with our footsteps echoed into the distance. We eventually reached a long row of dense foliage. In the absolute silence we pushed through some thick brush at the edge of a clearing and then stopped dead in our tracks.

Spread out before us, in the middle of this pristine wilderness, was a massive amusement park. Standard theme park music exploded around us—the hedge we stepped through had somehow been a perfect sound barrier.

A huge sign read, "TROUT LAND – Where Dreams Come True (If Your Dreams Involve Fish)." Next to the main sign was an advertisement from none other than the Count which read, "Trout Land sponsored by The Count's Heart-Stoppin' Chicken. Chicken, the Trout of the land."

There was an enormous parking lot filled with cars, and beyond that, the most bizarre theme park I'd ever seen. People in giant trout costumes were walking around, waving at visitors. There were signs flashing in neon light advertising fish-themed rides—a "Salmon Run Roller Coaster," a "Spinning Trout Carousel," and something called "The Fish Ladder of Death."

We looked at each other, shrugged, then started walking down an embankment that led to the edge of the parking lot. After another three miles we reached the entrance to the park. There were swarms of sweaty people moving this way and that, crying kids, old people with walkers, and seemingly healthy people in wheelchairs. Oh, and the strollers. Yes, the never-ending rows upon rows of strollers upon strollers.

Eventually, we found what looked to be the line to check in or buy tickets to the park.

"Are you sure this is what we reserved? How could this place even exist?" Bill asked.

"At this point I have no idea."

After about 30 minutes of waiting in a line that didn't move, Bill finally asked the person in front of us what the line was for. It turns out nobody knew what the line was for and the line to buy tickets and enter the park was a little bit further down from where we were.

By the time we finally made it into the park we were almost ready to leave. That's when we saw it. In the center of it all was a large artificial lake where people were fishing, surrounded by concession stands selling "Trout Dogs," "Fish and Chips Supreme," and "Salmon Smoothies." Also being sold because of the sponsorship was the Count's "Count 'em Up" buckets of chicken.

"What should we do?" Bill asked.

"I don't know," I said. "But I'm pretty sure this is where we fish."

As we stood there in shock, a familiar figure approached us. It was Harvey Stone, still dressed entirely in black, but now wearing a trout-shaped hat that someone had apparently forced on him.

"Ah, Jacob and William," he said in his fake Transylvanian accent. "Welcome to this… commercial abomination of the natural fishing experience."

"Harvey! What are you doing here?"

"I was lured here by promises of 'authentic fishing experiences,'" he said dramatically. "Instead, I find myself surrounded by costumed fish-people and mechanical trout that sing songs. It is… surprisingly entertaining, actually."

"How long have you been here?"

"Three days. I've ridden the Salmon Run seventeen times. The existential dread of plummeting toward earth while fish-themed music plays is oddly satisfying."

We walked around Trout Land for a bit, checked into the trout farm (which came with complimentary trout hats), and found our way to a shady fishing spot on the north side of the lake. Despite the absurdity of the setting, the fishing was quite good.

"I can't believe I'm saying this," Bill said, casting his line, "but this is kind of fun."

"The fish don't seem to mind the theme park," I agreed, pulling in my third trout of the morning.

Harvey was fishing nearby, somehow managing to make even this activity look gothic and brooding. "The fish understand suffering," he announced. "They appreciate authentic artistic expression, even in this commercialized hellscape."

We spent the morning fishing and then went to get lunch at "The Spawning Grounds Café," where everything on the menu was fish-themed. Harvey ordered something called "The Goth Trout Special"—apparently just regular trout dyed black.

As we sat eating our trout burgers and drinking "Stream Water Sodas," Bill brought up the subject I'd been dreading.

"Say," Bill said, "what about this Brett business?"

"What about it?"

"Were you ever in love with her?"

"Sure."

"And now she's with that Cohn character?"

"Was with him. Briefly."

"What's the deal with her, anyway? I mean, every guy who gets near her seems to end up… damaged."

I looked around to make sure no one was listening, then leaned in closer.

"You want to know the truth? I think Brett's cursed."

"Cursed?"

"Think about it. Every man who gets involved with her has something terrible happen to them. A few recent examples: There was Fabio Gustavo—famous model who was blown up during a fashion show. Paul Weinstein—stock trader who went bankrupt. Count Cholesterol—multiple heart attacks and his businesses failing one by one."

"And Cohn?"

"Torn ACL, head wounds, losing at everything he used to be good at. And that's just the beginning."

"But why would it still get worse for Cohn if he isn't even with her anymore? She went back to Mike, right?" Bill asked.

"Yes, she went back," I said. "But he still hasn't given up. He's still obsessed, stalking her. I mean, he wanted to stay back so he could hang out with Brett and Mike together. Talk about the ultimate third wheel. All this because he still thinks there is a chance with her. Until he gives that up I'm afraid it will only get worse."

Harvey, who had been eavesdropping, nodded gravely. "Ah yes, the beautiful woman who brings destruction. A classic gothic archetype. Very romantic, in a deeply tragic way."

"If the curse is so bad why are you seemingly doing ok?" Bill asked.

"I'll tell you exactly why because I think I finally figured it all out. The toe fungus that kept me from being with her. It only got worse after I met her but before we could get a chance to date. Luckily for me, this curse protected me. We were never together as she was always repulsed by the fungus. Ultimately, the fungus saved my life."

They were staring at me with amazement. I continued, "But just recently, I learned something important. Ever since I gave up all hope of being with her my toe fungus is slowly going away. Look!"

I took off my shoe and sock and showed them my foot. The fungus was almost non-existent.

"P.U!" Bill exclaimed while waving his hand. "Ok, we get it! You can put your shoe back on."

"The curse works differently on each person," I said. "But it always works."

"Fascinating," Harvey said. "Perhaps I should write a gothic poem about this. 'The Lady of Perpetual Doom' or something similar."

"Well, what about Mike?" Bill asked. "He seems okay, and he's engaged to her right?"

"I'm not so sure he's okay. After all, he drinks even more than we do—maybe the excessive alcohol is masking the curse's effects, or maybe *it is* the curse's effect."

We sat in silence for a few moments before I continued.

"And maybe there are things we don't know about him and his past. But what we do know is he's clearly a drunk, he has a beautiful fiancé that cheats on him weekly, and he's seemingly oblivious to it all. That doesn't sound like everything is normal to me. What I know for sure is that no one escapes the curse. Mike's just… on a longer timeline perhaps."

We all nodded in silent agreement.

We spent the afternoon trying various trout-themed rides. Harvey particularly enjoyed "The Tunnel of Scales," which was basically a haunted house but with fish instead of ghosts. Bill won a stuffed trout at the ring toss game. I managed to catch six more fish.

As the sun started to set, we sat by the lake watching the mechanical trout fountain show while eating trout-shaped cotton candy. We then found a good spot along one of the paths to watch the light parade at the end of the day. The parade included a fully lit up mascot of the park: Freddy Fish.

As the multitude of fish-themed floats passed by us we heard the Freddy Fish theme song. We stood there, arms around each other's shoulders, swaying, and singing as loudly as possible with our fish ale in our other hands:

"Freddy Fish, Freddy Fish,
You know he's the only fish for me.
Freddy Fish, Freddy Fish,
The only fish I'd want to be.
F-R-E-D-D-Y
F-I-S-H and me!"

"You know what?" Bill said. "This is the most relaxed I've seen you in months."

"I feel great," I agreed. "Giving up on Brett worked. The curse is reversing."

"And the fishing's not bad either," Harvey added. "Plus, the existential absurdity of this place speaks to my artistic soul."

We ended up staying at Trout Land for five days. Every morning we'd fish in the lake, spend the afternoons on the rides, watch the parade at night then on to playing cards with Harvey while he regaled us with increasingly elaborate gothic interpretations of the theme park's attractions.

There was no word from Cohn, no word from Brett and Mike. For five blissful days, it was just the three of us, some surprisingly good fishing, and the most ridiculous theme park in Spain.

On our last night, as we sat watching the trout parade, Bill raised his trout-shaped mug.

"To peaceful fishing trips," he said.

"To reversing the curse," I added.

"To the beautiful darkness that dwells within commercial fish-themed entertainment," Harvey said dramatically.

As we drank to that, I looked up toward the sky and saw dark clouds rolling in. I realized that I was dreading going back to Pamplona and whatever chaos Brett and the others would bring with them.

Chapter 13: She Has a Sister?

On the last morning there I went down to breakfast and Harvey Stone was already at the table, still wearing his Trout Land souvenir shirt and matching hat while somehow maintaining his gothic persona. He looked up from behind his dark sunglasses.

"Good morning, Jacob," he said dramatically. "A letter has arrived. I sense it brings… disturbance."

The letter was on my side of the table, leaning against a coffee-cup. My stomach immediately sank. I knew it was from my friends, which meant drama, chaos, or some combination of both. The peaceful Trout Land days were officially over.

I opened the letter with dread. It was dated Sunday, San Sebastian:

Dear Jake,

We got here Friday but passed out and missed multiple train stops. Then Cohn led us to the wrong train entirely, so we've been delayed for days. We're finally heading to Pamplona Tuesday. Also, we ran into Brett's sister Beth—didn't know she had one! She's coming to Pamplona for a few days before heading to San Sebastian to help at an orphanage. See you soon! -Michael

I stared at the letter. "Wait… She has a sister?"

"What?" Harvey asked.

"Brett has a sister."

Bill came down and I showed him the letter. "She has a sister?" he said.

We looked at each other and simultaneously asked, "I wonder what she looks like?"

"We need to get back to Pamplona," I told Harvey. "Our friends are there."

"Ah, you must return to the chaos," Harvey said dramatically. "I shall remain here; the fiesta has become so commercialized it has lost all authenticity."

"You're staying at Trout Land?" Bill asked. "But isn't it… commercialized?"

Harvey looked down at his Trout Land merchandise. "This is… different. This is ironic commercialization. Very gothic. Very authentic."

Just then, a girl came up with a telegram. I opened it with growing dread:

Buenos Dias, I come Thursday. PS, I was with Brett in San Sebastian just in case you forgot. -Robert

I crushed the telegram in my fist.

"Oh great," Bill said. "He's coming here? We need to leave immediately."

We debated sending a response but decided instead to tell the innkeeper that if they saw some weirdo in a leotard asking about us to tell him we'd gone to Pamplona.

We spent the last moments before we left reminiscing with Harvey about all the fun we had in the past week. We agreed to meet up later in Paris. Harvey gave each of us a Trout Land keychain as parting gifts. "May these protect you from the coming darkness," he said solemnly.

Bill and I braced ourselves and headed back to Pamplona.

We got into town late in the afternoon. The hotel sign read "Montoya's Hen House—Home of Champion Rooster Fighters." Montoya greeted us, but immediately I could tell something was wrong. He was shaking his head as he shook our hands.

"Your friends are here," he said with obvious disappointment. "Are they really your friends? Especially that Cohn guy—you know him? Because I've always known you to be an aficionado, but these people… I don't know about these people."

"They've never seen the Running of the Roosters or a Rooster Fight before," I explained. "But I promise to teach them to respect the roosters and fighters."

"The normal roosters are coming in tonight," Montoya said. "And tomorrow, the Supreme Roosters. They're a new breed—bigger, stronger, faster than normal fighting roosters. Anyone with true afición will appreciate their magnificence."

Afición means passion. Passion for roosters, passion for rooster fighters. All the good rooster fighters stayed at Montoya's Hen House. He kept pictures of all the rooster fighters who he thought had afición. Sometimes one would disgrace the sport with his behavior. At that point Montoya would take his picture down and burn it in the fireplace. Because I had afición, Montoya forgave me for my friends… for now.

Bill and I decided to check out our rooms first before meeting up with everyone. We were trying to delay the inevitable for as long as we could. I could tell Bill was uneasy about what the rooster unloading and fighting would be like.

"What's the rooster unloading like?" Bill asked nervously. "Do they kill the hens? I get queasy at the sight of blood."

"It should be fine," I said, though privately I was worried about these new super roosters.

Eventually, we headed down to the café.

There they were: Brett and Mike wearing touristy sombreros (Montoya was visibly not pleased), and Cohn wearing a shirt that said "I Dance, You Stare" in battery-powered letters that flashed on and off. He had an insufferably smug look on his face.

"How was your trip?" I asked.

"Cohn got us lost," Mike said. "Led us to completely the wrong train."

"How are your legs?" Bill asked Cohn.

"Getting better," Cohn said, though he was now wrapped in enormous amounts of ace bandages and carrying a cane. He was also wearing thick spectacles—apparently his vision was deteriorating too.

Bill and I exchanged glances. The curse was real and getting worse.

Brett looked stunning as usual. When she got up to greet us, waiters who caught glimpses of her dropped their plates and walked into each other. The staff and visitors were used to this occurrence by now and everyone carried on as if nothing had happened.

After greeting us Brett said, "I don't think you've met my sister, Beth."

That's when I noticed her—sitting quietly at the table. Beth was very attractive but dressed modestly; she wasn't wearing revealing clothing or trying to get attention like Brett. I was instantly smitten but tried to hide it. Brett watched me from the corner of her eye, as if she suspected something.

"Pleased to meet you," Beth said with a warm smile.

"The pleasure is all mine," I took her hand and kissed it in that old fashioned way. Brett looked at me through narrowed eyes.

"How did you all meet up?" I asked.

"I was passing through to San Sebastian when I found Mike and Brett passed out on a train station bench," Beth said. "Then I saw Cohn on the floor beside them. He was staring at Brett and eating some strange yellow substance from a jar."

"That was the great Beige Poupon," Cohn said proudly.

"I'd never seen anything like it," Beth said while looking at me and shrugging her shoulders. When our eyes locked it was as if she was saying to me, *are you really with these people*?

"But let me tell you a little bit about our sweet Beth over here," Brett said sarcastically, as she put her hand around Beth's shoulder. "She's on her way to help at an orphanage. Then she's vacationing in San Sebastian because she enjoys the peace and quiet. She doesn't like to drink or get into fights. Sometimes, she even carries a Bible—odd if you ask me."

"She also doesn't like to date countless numbers of men," Mike added. He was immediately elbowed by Brett.

"Oh, and she likes playing kids' games,"' Brett added. "You know, like Pokémon, board games…"

"Hey, we're the kids who like those games too!" I said, immediately feeling a deepening connection with Beth.

We continued talking and had a great meal. After a while, we all agreed to watch the rooster unloading. Beth said she wanted to visit the cathedral first and would meet us later. Of course, Cohn wouldn't leave Brett's side. He struggled to keep up because of his legs and use of the cane. Occasionally we would speed up our walking only to have him speed up his limping.

At the corrals, we found a good spot to watch. The chicken coops were being unloaded from trucks. As the workers lowered the coops to the ground we could see each stamped with a skull and crossbones symbol—some had one stamp, some two, some three.

"The stamps show how vicious and dangerous the rooster has been bred to be," I explained.

After waiting a while with no action, Cohn started whining like a child. "How long is this going to take? This is boring!"

I noticed that he wasn't even looking at the corral but was staring directly into a fence. He couldn't tell the difference because his eyesight was so bad, and his glasses were so dirty. I didn't care to correct him. Locals would pass by him staring and laughing; here was a grown man in a light up dance shirt with inch thick, dirty spectacles staring into a fence and complaining.

The hens were released first to calm the roosters. I leaned over the wall and could see dust being kicked up inside the coops. Strange, aggressive noises were coming from within—

more violent than I'd ever heard before. I'd been to numerous fiestas and unloading's but something felt different this time.

"This is boring!" Cohn exclaimed again, completely oblivious to the danger.

A horn sounded which was a warning that the coops would be opening. The first coop door was slowly opened. Just as the door was being opened a great force exploded against it from the other side. The handler got caught on the door and couldn't get away fast enough. He was immediately gored by the sharpened beaks of two vicious roosters. The crowd collectively gasped "Ouch!"

The roosters then proceeded to gore most of the hens before finally calming down.

"Boring!" Cohn started to say again, then Bill passed out from the blood.

I looked at Cohn then down at Bill. I looked up and caught Montoya's eye from across the corral. He was shaking his head in deep disappointment.

This was the first time I'd ever heard of someone being gored at an unloading before.

We carried Bill to a carriage and went to a café to continue our drinking streak. Bill came to after we poured some alcohol in his mouth.

"That was amazing!" Brett said.

"Boring," Cohn muttered. "I couldn't see anything anyway."

"Well, you were staring at the fence the entire time," I said.

"Is that why everything was green? Either way, it's no good being a hen," he added.

"Oh, I thought you'd like being a hen," Mike said nastily. "Laying bad eggs all the time. Here's Cohn dancing…" Mike stood up then strutted around like a chicken yelling, "Cluck, cluck, cluck."

He stopped then exploded about Cohn stalking them through San Sebastian. He started walking over to Cohn, his face red with anger.

"And then this guy shows up in San Sebastien following Brett around like a little prancing chihuahua," Mike said.

"But Brett was with me!" Cohn protested.

"Who cares? She's with everyone!" Mike shouted.

The entire café fell silent. Everyone stared at Brett, who put her head down.

"I'll dance you right into your grave, you drunk loser!" Cohn said, struggling to his feet with his cane.

"Fine! Let's dance!" Mike said.

"Okay, big guys," I said, breaking it up. "I know we're all pumped up from the roosters. Too much testosterone for Mike and too much… whatever flows through your body, Cohn."

Bill took Cohn outside to cool off. I watched him limp away with his cane and thick spectacles.

After they left, Mike tried to explain his anger. "Brett's had affairs before—almost weekly—but they never hang around like that or are that annoying. I'm almost ashamed she cheated on me with something like that."

"It's okay," Brett said. "It's over, and you still have me and your health, right?"

I thought to myself: *He won't have his health for long if he stays with you.*

After we finished our drinks we all walked to the hotel. On our way to our rooms, I ran into Montoya. He stared at me without expression and I knew it was because of my friends. I tried to make small talk to smooth over the situation.

"What do you think of the roosters?" I asked.

"The roosters seemed different this year," he said. "Almost… possessed. And those weren't even the Supreme Roosters."

"I had a strange feeling myself. Tell me, have you ever seen a goring at the unloading before? Or a rooster explode out of the coop like that?"

"In all my years I have never seen such a thing. And I've been to them all for the last 40 years."

That struck a nerve. *Oh no*, I thought. *Did I just bring the Brett curse to the festival?*

That evening, we all met for dinner, including Beth. It turned out to be surprisingly pleasant because I could talk to someone normal for once. We were getting along wonderfully. I noticed Cohn was just staring at Brett the entire time, occasionally taking off his thick glasses to clean them for a better view.

It was a calm dinner, but I couldn't shake a feeling of dread. The curse, the aggressive roosters, the immediate goring—too many things were adding up. The only thing putting me at ease was getting to know Beth. But I knew this peaceful moment wouldn't last long.

Chapter 14: Love Blooms and Fortunes Turn Dark

I don't know what time I got to bed, but for the first time in months, I was completely sober. I hadn't touched a drop all evening because I was so captivated by Beth. I remember undressing, putting on a bathrobe, and standing out on the balcony, thinking about how refreshing it was to talk to someone like her. I had only just met her and I already couldn't get her out of my mind.

I tried to read a book by Hemingway, but I couldn't concentrate. All I could think about was Beth—how she laughed at my crazy stories, how she didn't roll her eyes when I mentioned board games, how she actually seemed interested in having a real conversation instead of just complaining about not meeting enough millionaires. And how I felt when she touched my hand, and how—

I heard Brett and Cohn come up the stairs. THUNK. THUNK. THUNK. His cane was hitting each step so loudly it was waking up the entire hotel.

"Brett," I heard him whisper desperately outside her door. "Please, we need to talk."

"Robert, go to bed."

"But we're meant to be together! You understand my interpretive dance! No one else appreciates my artistic vision like you do!"

Brett laughed. "You're drunk, Robert. Maybe you should give Frances a call."

"I'm not drunk! I never get drunk! I only drink Beige Poupon smoothies now!"

"That's disgusting. Good night."

I heard Cohn's cane thumping as he continued up to his room, mumbling about how Brett was his true love.

For the first time, I actually laughed when I thought about Mike making fun of Cohn. I didn't even feel bad about it. I had finally found someone worth caring about, and Cohn's pathetic obsessions seemed even more ridiculous in comparison.

The next two days in Pamplona were surprisingly peaceful. The town was getting ready for the fiesta, and our group was getting along for once.

Beth suggested we go to church, which seemed like a perfectly normal thing to do. Brett decided to come too, though I wasn't sure why.

"I'll try being religious," Brett announced. "How hard could it be?"

We made it about ten minutes into the service before Brett started squirming.

"My skin is burning," she whispered urgently. "Something's wrong. I need to get out of here."

She practically ran outside, leaving Beth and me to finish the service in peace.

After church, Brett was waiting outside looking agitated. "That was horrible. Let's go see a fortune teller instead. Much more my style."

As we walked toward the gypsy camp, I noticed rustling in some nearby bushes. Suddenly, Cohn popped up casually, as if he'd been out for a pleasant stroll. Twigs were still stuck in his hair and his glasses were all fogged over.

"Oh, hello!" he said, brushing leaves off his Princeton varsity jacket. "Fancy running into you here! I was just… examining the local flora."

"Were you hiding in the bushes?" Beth asked.

"Hiding? No, no. I was doing interpretive dance inspired by nature. Very avant-garde. You wouldn't understand."

Beth and I looked at each other. I shrugged my shoulders and shook my head. She laughed.

The fortune teller was an old gypsy woman sitting in a colorful tent filled with crystals and burning incense. Her eyes were glazed over in a thin white film. You could see her white eyeballs moving around but couldn't tell exactly who or what she was looking at. It was giving me the creeps. Brett sat down eagerly while the rest of us waited outside.

The fortune teller began reading Brett's palm and then I heard a strange sound—it was like a shriek from another world, another dimension. I rushed back inside the tent and saw the teller's face—it was as pale as moonlight. She dropped Brett's hand as if it had burned her.

"No, no, no," she started mumbling. "Darkness… pure darkness…"

"What did you see?" Brett asked.

The fortune teller just kept mumbling in what sounded like a mixture of Spanish and ancient curses. She began frantically waving incense around Brett and began licking Himalayan salt while putting crystals on her stomach.

"What's wrong?" I asked.

The fortune teller looked at me with terror in her eyes. "Darkness," she whispered. "Pure darkness. She brings ruin to all who love her. The curse is strong with this one."

Brett came out of the tent annoyed. "Well, that was useless. She just kept mumbling nonsense."

"What did she say?" Cohn asked, still trying to casually brush twigs out of his hair.

"Nothing coherent," I said, though privately I was thinking the fortune teller had been remarkably accurate.

The rest of our time was surprisingly pleasant. Beth and I spent hours talking about books, games, and her work with orphanages. For the first time in years, I felt like I was having real conversations with someone who wasn't completely self-absorbed.

Even more surprisingly, no one was drinking that much. Bill was writing, Brett was distracted by shopping, and Cohn was too busy stalking Brett to be bothering me. For some reason, none of them seemed to understand that drinking was part of their problems, but as members of the "Lost Generation," apparently constant alcohol consumption was mandatory.

The only member of our group who was struggling during this time was Mike. Word had reached him about a crash at the London Stock Exchange. I remember seeing him one night downstairs at the bar by himself. He had his head on the table and in his hand was a newspaper. The main headline read,

"PANIC IN ENGLAND: MARKET CRASH CRUSHES INVESTORS."

"Are you all right, Mike?" I asked hesitantly.

He had been drinking heavily, and even lifting his head seemed to be a monumental task.

"I'm finished," he said, "finished…"

"Oh, come on Mike. There've been crashes before. The market will just go back up—you know what they say, 'buy low, sell high.'"

"You don't get it," he said, and then took another drink. He stared off into space and continued, "It was all borrowed money—I was leveraged to the hilt. The crash wiped me out."

His head dropped again onto the bar. Eventually, I got him up to bed. When I told Brett about it, she looked shocked and immediately began counting what was left in his wallet.

On our last evening before the fiesta began, Beth found me on the hotel balcony.

"I'm leaving tonight," she said quietly. "Before the festival begins."

My heart sank. "Why?"

"I don't think I should be here when things get… intense. Plus, the orphanage is expecting me."

"Of course," I said, trying to hide my disappointment. "That's very responsible of you."

We stood together on the balcony for a while, my hand around her waist as we watched the sunset together.

"Here," she said, handing me a piece of paper. "My phone number in San Sebastian. I'll only be there for a few weeks but call me if you stop by on your way back up to Paris."

I looked at the paper like it was made of gold. "I'd like that very much."

"And Jake? Be careful with your friends. I don't think they're very good for you."

After she left, I sat on the balcony thinking about how different the past few days had been. No major drama, no bleeding, no drinking (except Mike), no dance offs, no one passing out from interpretive dance injuries. Just normal, pleasant human interaction.

Tomorrow the fiesta would begin, bringing the Running of the Roosters, the Rooster Fights, and whatever chaos Brett's curse would unleash on Pamplona. But for now, I had Beth's phone number in my pocket and the first genuine hope I'd felt in months.

Even if I had to survive whatever disasters were coming, at least I knew there was someone normal in the world who might want to talk to me about things other than drinking. There were in fact people part of this generation who weren't "Lost."

I fell asleep clutching Beth's phone number like a lifeline. Tomorrow the fiesta would begin. But tonight, I had hope. And sometimes, that's enough to get you through whatever madness awaits.

Chapter 15: Fiesta Begins and Roosters Strike

At noon on Sunday, the 6th of July, the fiesta exploded. There is no other way to describe it. Explosions ripped through the sky marking the beginning of the fiesta known by the locals as the San Fermin festival but known by the tourists as Chicken Gras.

The explosions weren't limited to the chicken themed fireworks. The town's population exploded overnight; the number of people made walking around feel like you were swimming upstream. It was now near impossible to find places to sit at the various cafés and restaurants in towns.

I made my way through a large crowd down to the café where Cohn and Bill were sitting at one of the cast-iron tables. Just as I sat down the first part of the fiesta started. I could see large floats in the horizon coming toward us. The street was now filled with dancers and various performers.

The café itself had been stripped for action like a battleship preparing for war. Iron tables took up every available inch of space and the waiters were in non-stop "sell" mode. Cohn was wearing what appeared to be a new interpretive dance costume under his regular clothes—I could see the edge of a sequined leotard peeking out from his collar.

"What are you drinking?" I asked.

"Sherry," Cohn said, while simultaneously critiquing the nearby street performers. "Look at that footwork! Completely wrong! Their arm positioning is amateur at best. I could teach them proper interpretive movement if they'd listen."

"Maybe you should go show them," Bill suggested with a grin.

"I would, but my knees are too swollen," Cohn said, adjusting his thick spectacles. "And my new prescription glasses make depth perception challenging for complex choreography."

Before the waiter could bring my drink, more rockets exploded above the square. What followed was absolute chaos—a full Chicken Gras parade featuring massive chicken and rooster-themed floats, dancers in elaborate feathered costumes, and people throwing eggs in every direction.

SPLAT! A raw egg hit Cohn directly in the face, yolk dripping down his Princeton varsity jacket.

"This is completely inauthentic!" he yelled, wiping egg from his thick glasses. "I've had enough, swollen knees or not. The traditional San Fermin dance requires much more sophisticated arm movements! Watch!"

Cohn stood up and began demonstrating what he considered proper festival dancing, flailing his arms in elaborate patterns while egg yolk continued to drip from his chin. The crowd stopped to stare.

"Is that an American?" asked a confused local.

"Robert, sit down!" Bill called, but Cohn was in his element now.

"You see, the authentic movement starts from the core!" Cohn shouted to anyone who would listen, spinning awkwardly on his injured knees. "Like this! One, two, three, interpretive leap!"

He attempted a jump and immediately collapsed, his knee giving out. Several festival dancers helped him back to his chair while he continued to critique their technique.

"Your timing is off," he told his rescuers. "And you're not feeling the music in your souls."

Cohn was placed back into his seat just as the first floats were coming into view. The first float that passed was extraordinary. On the front was a huge flashing neon read sign that read, "The Count is Back." The float was a fifty-foot mechanical rooster being ridden by Count Cholesterol, who was surrounded by a complete medical team. Two nurses were monitoring his heart rate while a doctor adjusted his oxygen mask between his announcements to the crowd.

"LADIES AND GENTLEMEN!" the count wheezed into a megaphone. "WELCOME TO CHICKEN GRAS! SPONSORED BY THE COUNT'S HEART-STOPPIN' CHICKEN! COCK-A-DOODLE YES!"

He was throwing chicken nuggets to the crowd while struggling to stay upright on his enormous rooster. Every few minutes he would clutch his chest and the medical team would rush to his aid.

"Oh boy," I said sarcastically to Bill. "The count is back."

"And apparently sponsoring the whole fiesta," Bill replied, watching the count's float wobble dangerously as he had what appeared to be another mild heart attack.

"NUGGETS FOR EVERYONE!" the count shouted, then immediately collapsed onto his medical team. "QUICK! THE DEFIBRILLATOR!"

The crowd cheered as electrical jolts could be seen reviving the count, who immediately stood up and continued throwing nuggets.

"This is the most absurd thing I've ever seen," I said.

"Wait," Bill pointed. "Look at Brett."

As more floats passed, I noticed Brett was accumulating an impossible number of beaded necklaces. Every single person who caught sight of her immediately threw their beads in her direction.

"I can't… lift my arms," Brett gasped under the weight of 100's of heavy necklaces. "I can barely breathe."

"Mike, over here!" I yelled.

"Help!" Brett called weakly. "I'm being crushed by beads!"

We had to form a human chain to remove enough necklaces so she could move again. Bill, Mike, and I worked for ten minutes just to free her arms.

"How does this always happen to you?" Mike asked, pulling off strand after strand.

"I don't know!" Brett said. "I didn't ask for any of this!"

That's when the festival dancers noticed her. Despite Cohn's continued criticism from his chair ("No, no! You're supposed to leap first, then spin! And where's the emotional expression?"), they formed a perfect circle around Brett and began their traditional dance.

"Your ankles aren't aligned!" Cohn shouted at the dancers. "And you're not projecting your inner truth!"

The dancers ignored him completely and began lifting Brett above their heads while maintaining their intricate steps.

Then something completely surreal happened. From somewhere down the road, a massive float appeared featuring a giant statue that looked exactly like Brett—same hair, same face, same expression. The dancers placed the real Brett right next to her statue double.

"How is this even happening?" I asked no one in particular. "How did they make a statue of her? She's been here—what two days? Have you been here before?" I asked as I turned to her.

"No, this is the first time I've ever come down here," she said. "Maybe they've been waiting all this time for perfection like this to be realized."

"Maybe they have a really good sculptor," Bill suggested.

"Or maybe this whole town is cursed," I said, thinking about the fortune teller's warning.

The Brett float, complete with Brett herself and her mysterious statue, proceeded directly to the largest wine shop in town. The crowd followed like she was the Pied Piper, and soon the entire building was packed with revelers.

"Drinks for everyone!" someone shouted.

"On the house!" yelled another voice.

It was only day one of the fiesta, but within an hour we'd consumed what looked like a week's worth of alcohol. Even the locals were shocked.

"Señor," the bartender said nervously to me, "I've worked festivals for twenty years. At this rate, there won't be enough alcohol in all of Spain to survive the week."

"How much have we drunk?" I asked.

"You personally? About three bottles of wine. Your friends? I stopped counting after the fifteenth bottle."

I looked around. Brett was holding court in the center of the room, still wearing about fifty beads. Mike was singing what appeared to be a drinking song in a language I didn't recognize. Bill was attempting to learn traditional Spanish dances from locals who kept correcting his form. And Cohn was passed out in a corner, Beige Poupon had somehow leaked all over him from a jar in his pocket.

"Is he… marinating himself?" Brett asked, pointing at Cohn.

"I think the Beige Poupon container cracked when he fell," I said.

"He smells like a sandwich," Mike observed.

"Should we wake him up?" Bill asked.

"Let him sleep," I said. "He'll just start critiquing everyone's drinking technique."

I decided to go buy a wineskin for the week ahead. After all, there's always a need to have something to hold more wine. The first shop I found had a proprietor who was eager to demonstrate his product quality.

"Watch this, señor!" he said proudly, inflating a large leather bag. "I will show you how strong!"

He jumped on the inflated wineskin with both feet. The bag exploded with tremendous force, sending him flying across the shop and covering him in leather fragments and wine stains.

"AY, CARAMBA!" he screamed, clutching what appeared to be a dislocated shoulder.

"I think I'm good here," I said, backing toward the door as other customers rushed to help the injured proprietor.

At the next shop, the proprietor started to demonstrate the same jumping test.

"That's okay!" I said quickly. "I trust you, it's definitely good!"

"You sure? I like to show customers—"

"NO! No jumping necessary. I believe in your craftsmanship."

"Eight pesetas," he said proudly. "Very cheap price for such quality!"

"Great, I'll take two."

As soon as I left his shop with my wineskins, I saw a large sign across the street: "PREMIUM WINESKINS - 5 PESETAS - GUARANTEED NOT TO EXPLODE!"

"Doh!" I said out loud.

"First time in Spain?" asked a passing local.

"You could say that."

When I returned to the wine shop, the party had somehow intensified. Someone had set up what appeared to be a limbo contest using a bar decorated with chicken feathers. Brett was being serenaded by a mariachi band that had appeared from nowhere. Mike was doing shots with a group of Spanish farmers who were teaching him curse words. Bill was still dancing, now wearing a traditional Spanish hat someone had given him.

And Cohn was awake, still covered in Beige Poupon, now lecturing a group of confused locals about the proper way to conduct a wine tasting.

"You must swirl the wine exactly seven times," he was saying, completely serious. "And hold the glass at a forty-five-degree angle to appreciate the color properly."

The Spanish locals were nodding politely while exchanging glances that clearly said, "Is this American insane?"

"Also," Cohn continued, "you should pair this wine with Beige Poupon to enhance the flavor profile. Here, try some." He offered them his leaking jar.

"Roberto," said one local diplomatically, "perhaps you should clean yourself first?"

"This is part of the authentic wine experience," Cohn insisted. "The Beige Poupon marinade enhances the palate."

By evening, we somehow made it back to the hotel for dinner. The prices had doubled for the fiesta, and several new courses had been added. By the time we were ready to head up to our rooms it was three in the morning. I resolved to stay up all night to watch the Running of the Roosters at dawn.

"I want to stay awake to watch the roosters but I don't know if I'll make it," I announced to the group and then yawned.

"I just drank 40 oz...of coffee," said Bill proudly. "Someone should witness the carnage."

"It's not carnage," Mike protested. "It's tradition!"

"Have you seen those roosters?" Brett asked. "They look absolutely murderous."

"They're just big chickens," Cohn said dismissively. "How dangerous could they be?"

Around four in the morning, I finally fell asleep in my room despite my best intentions. The rest of the group had stayed awake and had found a place to watch the Running of the Roosters just above the street level.

At around six in the morning, I was awakened by a rocket that sounded exactly like a rooster's morning crow. The rocket announced the roosters had been released. I grabbed my jacket and stumbled out to the balcony alone.

Down below, I could see the crowd running around the corner from the direction of the released roosters. Behind the running crowd came the first batch of roosters—supposedly the "normal" ones. But these birds were huge, larger than a regular rooster, with beaks that had been sharpened to razor points. Clearly hormones and steroids were used—clearly not free range.

I saw a few runners skidding in the dirt, narrowly escaping the sharpened beaks as the fowl missed their target. Many roosters had their beaks stuck in the fence and had to be pried off by handlers. Other than that, the roosters seemed more coordinated than I had ever seen before.

"Help me," I heard someone scream from the street. "They're enormous!"

In the distance, I saw eyes glowing red in the morning light and flashes of speed and aggression.

In the middle of the chaos a drunk man jumped over the fence onto the street. He was flapping his arms like a chicken and kicking his feet back. At first the roosters were just running by him on either side. He then started to taunt them.

"You're nothing more than taco filling!" he said to them as they ran whizzing by.

"Don't be such a chicken, chicken!" he laughed. "Now I'm going to get me one of you fatties for breakfast."

I couldn't help thinking this seemed like a poor strategy for getting food, even for a drunk person.

He pulled out a knife and started running *towards* the roosters. Then from somewhere in the distance, from one of the cages labeled "Supreme Roosters," we heard a bone-chilling shriek. At that exact moment all the roosters who had not yet made it to the arena corrals stopped in their tracks. They circled the drunk man, slowly closing in on him, step by four-toed scratching step.

We heard another shriek, and the man was immediately attacked by roosters pecking with frenzied intensity. It was how one might imagine a pack of velociraptors attacking their prey. There was no hope for the man; he came for fun but the roosters came for revenge.

"GET A DOCTOR!" someone screamed.

Handlers jumped over the fences with large cattle prods and were quickly able to disperse the roosters to the corral. What was left in the street was a crumpled lifeless form, shredded beyond recognition. It reminded me of something from World War I.

As the medical staff surrounded the man, the crowd started to disperse. The music started back up. Now mind you, this wasn't completely unusual. Runners being gored at past fiestas had happened before. It was usually some drunk person trying to impress their friends. But to me, the most disturbing part was the roosters' behavior.

The roosters seemed fairly normal at first but when threatened that all changed. And what was that shrieking squawk? It was like an order that commanded them. After the order they seemed to be working together and coordinated their final assault like a military unit.

"This isn't natural," I said to myself.

I sat in an almost hypnotic trance watching as the street was slowly cleaned up and normal fiesta activities resumed.

I was still recovering from the shock of the morning when Cohn stumbled into the room wearing an "I Love Brett" bracelet and a ridiculous hen-shaped tourist hat he'd apparently bought during the festivities.

"Did you see the show?" I asked.

"Yes, but I was too busy being heartbroken to pay proper attention," he said dramatically. "My soul is crushed by unrequited love."

"Did you see anyone get hurt?"

"Who cares if anyone was hurt?" Cohn said, adjusting his thick glasses. "I'm hurt inside because of Brett. That's the only thing that matters. Physical pain is nothing compared to the anguish of a rejected artist."

"Robert, someone was literally gored by giant roosters."

"Were they? I didn't notice. I was composing an interpretive dance piece about emotional suffering. Want to see it?"

"No."

"It's called 'The Lament of the Unappreciated Dancer.' I think it captures my current situation perfectly."

I turned away from him and went back to bed. *Good talk*, I thought. *Good talk*.

Everyone slept in until just after noon, which wasn't surprising given our lifestyle of drinking all night, sleeping until noon, and complaining about everything. It was a hard life we'd chosen for ourselves.

At lunch, we met to prepare for the afternoon's rooster fights. The entire town was buzzing with excitement and terror after the morning's carnage.

Mike was already three drinks deep and flipping through the newspaper, looking for stock quotes from England. "I'm ruined… I'm ruined," he kept muttering.

"I still think I'll be bored," Cohn announced, spreading Beige Poupon on his bread. "These provincial entertainments rarely meet my artistic standards."

"There's going to be actual fighting," Bill said. "With blood."

"I've seen blood before," Cohn replied. "During my dance performances, I've bled for my art. Literally. Remember when I scratched my arm expressing the liquidity of water?"

Brett wondered aloud if she'd be able to get through the fights. "Will there be anyone attractive to look at? That usually helps me focus."

Before we could answer, Bill and I saw Montoya walking towards us. He looked more serious than I'd ever seen him.

"Come," Montoya said urgently. "You must meet Pedro Romero. But first, you must promise me something."

"What?" I asked.

"Do not let your friends corrupt this boy. He is the *greatest* rooster fighter I have ever seen, and he is only nineteen years old. If your woman friend gets her hands on him…" Montoya shook his head. "Promise me you will protect him."

"I'll try," I said, though I already knew it was hopeless.

"Try is not enough. You are an aficionado—you understand what is at stake. This boy could be the greatest who ever lived. But if he gets involved with your friends…"

Montoya led us upstairs to Pedro's room. As we climbed the stairs, the distinct smell of fried chicken grew stronger.

"Is someone cooking?" Bill asked.

"Count Cholesterol is sponsoring the boy," Montoya explained with obvious distaste. "His company logo is on Pedro's cape. It pays the bills, but it smells terrible."

We knocked on the door and entered. The room reeked of fried chicken, and there in the corner sat Count Cholesterol, still connected to a portable oxygen tank and monitoring equipment. He was eating chicken nuggets while reviewing sponsorship contracts.

"Ah!" wheezed the count when he saw us. "Jake! Bill! Come to see my investment?"

Pedro Romero stood in the center of the room, and he was without question the most attractive young man I'd ever seen. He looked like he'd been born to fight roosters—calm, confident, and completely unaware of his own beauty.

"You go to the rooster-fight," Pedro said in English.

"You know English," I said, feeling like an idiot.

"No," he answered with a smile that could stop traffic.

I glanced at Montoya and realized with growing dread that Brett was going to be all over this kid. There was no way to protect him from what was coming.

"Good luck today," I told Pedro.

"Mucha suerte," Bill added.

Count Cholesterol struggled to his feet. "The boy's going to be great! Great for business! I've got promotional plans—Pedro Romero's Rooster-Fighting Chicken Nuggets! Pedro's Poultry Family Meal! The possibilities are endless!"

He immediately clutched his chest and sat back down heavily.

"Sir, your heart rate is elevated," said one of his nurses.

"It's just excitement about the profit margins," the count wheezed.

We left Pedro to his preparations and went to collect our tickets for the fights.

At the arena, the atmosphere was electric but ominous. Word had spread about the morning's goring. The element of danger heighted everyone's excitement. The first day's fights were about to begin. There were three matadors fighting that day with Pedro Romero being the last.

The arena's electronic scoreboard lit up: "MATADORS: 0, ROOSTERS: 0."

Below that, a timer showed: "ROOSTER RELEASE: UNO... DOS... TRES"

I had briefly explained some of the rules of Rooster Fighting to my friends but added a quick reminder to them all:

"Watch the timer. Every thirty seconds a rooster is released until there are three roosters against the matador. The crowd will yell, 'UNO!', 'DOS!', 'TRES!'. The matadors try to give the crowd a good show until after the third rooster is released. At that point he'll most likely draw his sword and kill them."

The first matador entered the ring confidently. He was an experienced matador with 200 successful rooster fights under his belt. He bowed to the crowd and then readied himself.

"UNO!"

The first rooster bolted out of the cage running straight for the matador. The matador gracefully evaded the first lunging attack with his cape, the crowd applauded.

"DOS!"

Two roosters now attacked the matador's cape running from one end of the arena to another. The matador would shift his cape from side to side in graceful movements that looked like a well-choreographed dance that made Cohn jealous.

"He has a couple of good moves," Cohn admitted.

"TRES!"

As soon as this rooster was released we heard the same shriek as we did that morning, coming from the same cage in the distance. The attacks from that point on were different, coordinated, intelligent, and impossible to defend. The matador didn't stand a chance and within minutes, he was dead. The crowd gasped in horror.

"MATADORS: 0, ROOSTERS: 1."

"Is that normal," Bill said.

"Definitely not normal," I replied. I looked at Brett who was looking at her nails.

"They do serve alcohol here, right?" she asked.

"Evidently they do," I replied and gestured to Mike who somehow found where to get commemorative beer mugs that read, "Big Enough to Quench a True Matador." He had about five empty ones laying around him.

"Woohoo! Who's the chicken now?" he yelled to no one in particular. "Also, can I borrow a twenty from any of you?"

I saw Montoya from across the arena. He was talking to Pedro, preparing him with some new moves. He looked at me and then quickly looked away.

The second matador, even more well known than the first, took his spot in the center of the arena.

"UNO!"

The first rooster bolted out and it was the same pattern as before. It seemed normal at first. When you looked at it, you didn't get the impression of impending death but rather of impending lunch.

"DOS!"

The second rooster, in a trail of dust, skidded into the arena. Again, they both seemed manageable. In fact, if the matador were to draw his sword at this point he would have been able to dispatch both of them.

"TRES!"

This is when it changed. Again, a piercing squawk from the distance.

What was that, I thought.

And after the squawk the matador lasted slightly longer than the first one but met the same fate. The roosters weren't just fighting—they were evaluating the matador's weaknesses in real time and executing a perfect attack.

"MATADORS: 0, ROOSTERS: 2."

During the intermission Brett and Mike went to the concession stands for drinks. Bill and I agreed to go and get food.

"Hey Cohn, what do you want to eat?" Bill asked.

"Maybe a Filet Mignon. Don't forget the Beige Poupon," Cohn replied while cleaning his glasses with his extra thick sweater.

"Ok, one chicken dog for Cohn," I said.

"No Jake…" Cohn started as we walked away. "Don't forget the Poupon!!!"

After getting food for everyone and we met back in our seats.

Pedro Romero was next. He made his way to the center of the arena and for the first time that day Brett was paying attention.

"Wowza! Who's the dreamboat?" she asked.

Mike looked at her then at Pedro then back at her. You could tell by the expression on his face he knew what was coming.

Cohn looked at Mike then at Pedro then at her. You could tell by the expression on his face that he didn't know what was coming.

"That dreamboat is Pedro Romero," I said. "He's only 19 and already the best rooster fighter to come out of Spain. Hands off!"

"I likey," she said with that look in her eyes I knew so well.

"Promise me you'll leave him alone," I said. "I vouched for us with Montoya."

"Montoya, Monshmoya… fine I'll leave him alone," she sighed.

Mike looked relieved…kind of. And Cohn still looked as annoying as usual. He was busy finding everything wrong with the food we brought him.

"Are you sure this is cooked all the way?" I heard him ask Bill.

When the music started we all stopped talking and gave our attention to Pedro.

"UNO!"

The first rooster was no problem for a matador like Pedro. He put on an impressive show.

"DOS!"

Again, Pedro was in full control. Fully focused on the task at hand. At one with his art.

"TRES!"

Three roosters began zig zagging and attacking in unpredictable lunges. Pedro was unphased and was single handedly stealing the show.

Then the piercing squawk.

Here we go, I thought.

What followed was the most incredible display of skill I'd ever witnessed. Pedro seemed to anticipate every move the roosters would make. He danced around them with grace and precision, his cape work flawless, his timing perfect. The crowd was mesmerized.

"He's incredible," I said to Bill.

"I've never seen anything like it," Bill replied.

Even the roosters seemed to respect Pedro's skill. At one point they stopped and looked at each other; if they had shoulders they would have shrugged them. They fought him with honor rather than their usual murderous frenzy.

Pedro slowly tired the roosters out. Their attacks became easier to time, their lunges slower than before.

Pedro pulled out his sword. He made three well timed swings and all three roosters lost their heads. The crowd erupted in cheers. The roosters' bodies were immediately thrown on a huge outdoor grill.

The PA announcer's voice came on through the speakers: "Remember folks, if the matadors score 5 or more today everyone wins free chicken nuggets courtesy of The Count's Heart-Stoppin' Chicken!"

"MATADORS: 3, ROOSTERS: 2."

The crowd started chanting: "ENCORE! ENCORE! PEDRO! PEDRO!"

Pedro bowed. He then motioned to the handlers to open the remaining cages of the "normal" roosters. One by one he scored more kills until the grill was filled to the max.

"MATADORS: 10, ROOSTERS: 2."

Pedro bowed as the crowd threw roses and cheered. I caught Montoya's eye. He nodded approvingly as if to say, *see what I mean? This guy is the real deal.* I nodded back.

After the fights, we fought our way through the crowd to a café. The moment we sat down, I could see that look in Brett's eyes—she was obviously smitten.

"That Pedro is quite something," she said dreamily while doodling Pedro's name over and over again on a hotel notepad. "He's much more impressive than those other amateurs."

Cohn, still wearing his hen hat and covered in dried Beige Poupon, perked up jealously.

"I could be a rooster fighter too if that's what you want, Brett," he said desperately. "I have excellent reflexes from my interpretive dance training. I could probably be better than him."

Everyone at the table burst into laughter.

"Robert," Mike said, wiping tears from his eyes, "you passed out during the parade because you got hit with an egg."

"That was different," Cohn protested. "I was caught off guard. In the ring, I would be prepared. I could incorporate my dance moves to confuse the roosters."

"You can barely walk with your injured knees," Brett pointed out.

"Pain is just another form of artistic expression," Cohn declared. "I would turn my suffering into beauty."

Mike was laughing so hard he nearly fell off his chair. "Robert, you'd be dead in thirty seconds."

"I don't think Brett's interested in rooster fighters anyway," Bill said diplomatically.

We all looked at Brett, who was still staring off in the distance, a dreamy expression on her face.

"Oh no," I said quietly.

Mike, oblivious to the danger, raised his glass. "To rooster fighting! And to young Pedro, who made it look easy!"

I raised my glass but couldn't shake the feeling that we'd just witnessed the beginning of Pedro's downfall. The curse was spreading, and there was nothing any of us could do to stop it.

The rooster-fight on the second day was even better than the first. Brett wanted to sit up close so we upgraded to better seats. We were all able to get seats in the second row except for Cohn. He sulked all the way up to the last row of the arena, Bill and I almost died laughing at each step he took.

Pedro stole the show and was already a legend who grew in popularity with each fight. Two other matadors were killed on the second day. The roosters seemed to be growing more bold, more vicious with each fight. The shrieks from the other cages continued and you could tell the roosters were clearly trying to zone in on Pedro, seeking revenge for the roosters he killed in the fights.

His style was like none I had ever seen. On several occasions he seemed to stop time and dodge multiple attacks from multiple angles. I kept remarking to Brett about his technique, she kept remarking about how good he looked in those pants.

"I've never seen him look bad in those pants," she said. "And wowza, just look at him!"

Oh boy, here we go, I thought.

He killed another 10 roosters that day. At the end of the fights I looked in the direction of where those piercing squawks came from. I could have sworn I saw two red eyes glowing in one of the cages far off in the distance. And if they were eyes they were staring right at Pedro.

After it was over we went out and struggled through the crowd, eventually finding our way to the café.

"I think we all need a drink after that," Mike said.

"You read my mind," Brett agreed.

I'm not a doctor or anything but after a day of drinking I'm not sure that the next thing we *needed* was another drink but I was too tired to fight it. After all, we wouldn't be the "Lost Generation" if we didn't lose ourselves in drinking.

We skipped the Rooster Fights the next day as Pedro wasn't going to fight. We heard the fights didn't go so well. Montoya told me that no matadors survived that day. But even through all the carnage the fiesta kept up, all day and all night.

Through all the noise, there were times when I could hear the distinctive shriek coming from the distance. Barely audible at first, until I could hear nothing else—and then silence so abrupt it was deafening. It was the Silence of the Birds.

As I drifted to sleep that night, I had one of the most vivid dreams I could remember. I was a child on my family's farm. It was nighttime and I heard shrieks. I walked outside toward the sound, which was coming from a large barn directly behind the house.

I would hear a loud shriek, then a THWACK! Then silence. This continued as I walked closer. The barn door was cracked, light illuminating around the edges.

I slowly peered inside. THWACK! A chicken head flew directly toward me, hitting the door and narrowly missing my face. A figure with a large knife turned toward me—the body of a chicken slumped against a wooden stump.

It was my dad, culling chickens for market. He was wearing a strange mask with slits around the mouth, making him look like some kind of deranged serial killer.

"Do you hear the silence?" he said in a thick, raspy voice. "The silence of the birds?"

The shrieking started again and I ran. I ran as fast as I could—through a corn field, through a forest, somehow through a desert. I turned around only to see my father right behind me, now dressed in patched skins of the chickens he'd slaughtered.

"Don't you hear it?" he said again. "Embrace it, my son. Embrace the silence of the birds." He laughed and laughed as my dream faded into darkness.

I awoke in a cold sweat. *Wow*, I thought. *I really need to quit drinking.*

Chapter 16: Vanity, Destiny and Montoya Weeps

In the morning it was raining. A fog had come over the mountains from the sea, and you couldn't see the tops of the mountains. The plateau was dull and gloomy, and the shapes of the trees and houses looked ominous, like something out of a horror movie. I walked out beyond the town to look at the weather. The bad weather felt heavy with foreboding.

The flags in the square hung wet and limp from the white poles, and the banners sagged against the front of the houses. The rain drove everyone under the arcades and made pools of water in the square. The streets were wet, dark, and eerily quiet, yet the fiesta kept going without pause. It was only driven under cover, by some unstoppable force.

But something felt different about this rain. It wasn't just weather—there was an electric tension in the air, as if nature itself was preparing for something terrible. The locals kept glancing nervously at the sky and muttering about "los gallos supremos"—the Supreme Roosters—that were arriving today.

In the rooster fighting arena all the flags were at half mast, dripping from the rain and hanging lifeless as a symbolic gesture for all the matadors lost in the fiesta so far.

"I've never seen roosters like these," I heard one old man tell another. "They're not natural. They're bred for killing, not fighting."

The rain was also causing another problem. Every bar and café in town was dealing with increasingly drunk and paranoid customers who were convinced their drinks were being watered down.

"This wine tastes like rainwater!" Mike was shouting from inside the Café Gallo Borracho. "Are you trying to sober us up? We're paying customers!"

"Señor, please," the waiter pleaded, "the wine is not watered down. It is the same wine as always."

"Then why does it taste different?" Brett demanded. "We're not paying for diluted drinks!"

"Right!" Mike said and then continued in a low voice, *"In fact, I'm not paying at all."*

The poor waiters were running around frantically, trying to convince increasingly belligerent tourists that their alcohol hadn't been tampered with while simultaneously mopping up puddles of rainwater that kept forming near the windows.

I left the chaos and went back to the hotel to get shaved for dinner. I was halfway through shaving when there was a knock on my door.

"Come in," I called.

Montoya walked in, looking more serious than I'd ever seen him.

"How are you?" he said.

"Fine," I said. "Wet day."

"No roosters today. Too much rain for anything."

"Right. Just drinking and complaining about watered-down wine."

"Where are your friends?"

"Over at the Gallo Borracho, accusing waiters of conspiracy."

Montoya didn't smile. He looked deeply troubled.

"Look," he said, "I need to talk to you about Pedro."

I continued shaving, waiting for whatever bad news was coming.

"He's been invited to a party tomorrow night," Montoya continued. "Some American magazine people. They want to nominate him for 'World's Most Interesting Man' and 'World's Most Attractive Man' for Human Magazine."

I nearly cut myself with the razor. "What?"

"They're doing some kind of international feature. Pedro would be on magazine covers all over the world. Famous beyond just Rooster Fighting."

"You're not going to let him go, are you?"

"That's just it—I don't know if I can stop him. He's been looking at himself in mirrors more and more. Yesterday I caught him practicing poses. And with these Supreme Roosters coming tomorrow…" Montoya shook his head gravely.

I put down my razor. "Oh yes, the Supreme Roosters."

"Los gallos supremos. Jake, in forty years of rooster fighting, I've never seen birds like these. They're enormous, completely black, with red eyes and beaks sharpened to razor points. They move like shadows and attack with the precision of trained assassins. Two handlers were killed just unloading them from the trucks."

"And when is Pedro going to fight them?"

"Soon. And I'm afraid… I'm afraid he's getting distracted. The magazine attention, the mirrors, and now your woman friend keeps asking about him. A rooster fighter needs complete focus, especially with these creatures."

I finished washing my face and looked at Montoya in the mirror. His usually cheerful expression was replaced with genuine fear.

"Don't give Pedro the message about the magazine party," I said.

"You think that will help?"

"It's a start. But Montoya, you have to keep him away from my friends. Especially Brett. She's… she has a way of destroying men."

"I know about your friends," Montoya said grimly. "That dancing one follows her around like a sick puppy, and she collects men like trophies. But Pedro is young and beautiful and successful. He thinks he's invincible."

"Just promise me you'll try to keep them apart."

"I'll try. But you know how these things go. The more you tell a young man to stay away from a beautiful woman…"

After Montoya left, I tried to find my friends. Following a trail of empty wine bottles and stressed-out waiters wasn't difficult—they'd apparently been to at least six different establishments, leaving chaos in their wake.

"These people drink like they're trying to drain Spain dry," one exhausted waiter told me. "And they keep demanding we prove our wine isn't watered down by bringing them unopened bottles, then they drink those too!"

I finally found them back at the hotel's downstairs dining room. I arrived just as Bill was finishing what appeared to be a joke.

"...and, that's not how you shine shoes!" Bill announced with a flourish.

The entire table erupted in laughter. Even Cohn was giggling, which was disturbing. They were all so drunk that the simple act of sitting upright seemed to require enormous concentration.

I looked over and saw that Count Cholesterol was slumped in a corner chair, his portable oxygen tank wheezing regularly. He appeared to be unconscious, but occasionally he would mumble something about "profit margins" and "chicken nugget futures."

As I stood there watching this circus, I noticed Pedro Romero sitting at a nearby table. Pedro caught my eye and waved me over.

I left my friends—who didn't even notice my departure—and joined Pedro's table. He was sitting with one of the most famous rooster critics in all of Spain.

"How are you feeling about tomorrow?" I asked.

"Confident," Pedro said with that easy smile. "I've been preparing for months."

The critic, a small nervous man, shook his head. "I've seen these Supreme Roosters. I'm officially retiring from criticism after this. I can't even watch what's going to happen."

"Come on," Pedro laughed. "They're just big roosters. I've never met a rooster I couldn't handle."

"Pedro," I said, trying to find the right words, "listen, about my friends—"

"Don't worry, Jake. I know you're looking out for me."

"You don't understand. The woman especially. She's—"

"It's fine. Women are women. I can handle myself."

"Pedro, you really need to listen to me. She's cursed. Every man who gets involved with her—"

"Cursed?" Pedro looked amused.

Before I could explain, Brett's voice cut through the dining room like a knife.

"Yoo-hoo! Over there! What are you two boys plotting? Care to introduce me to your friend, Jake?"

Here we go again, I thought.

Pedro and I stood up and joined the group. Mike was in the middle of a drunken performance, yelling "Roosters are just chickens! Bawk! Bawk!" while doing an elaborate chicken dance that involved flapping his arms and pecking at invisible corn on the floor.

"Tell 'em, Jake!" Mike shouted. "Tell 'em roosters are just big chickens!"

Brett was staring at Pedro with the same intensity Cohn usually reserved for her. In fact, they formed a bizarre triangle of obsession: Cohn staring longingly at Brett, Brett staring hungrily at Pedro, and Pedro… Pedro was staring at himself in a large mirror on the dining room wall, admiring his profile.

"I like your pants, pretty boy!" Mike continued shouting. "Brett thinks you've got nice pants too! Don't you, Brett?"

"Mike, please," Brett said, never taking her eyes off Pedro.

I introduced everyone. "Pedro, this is Robert Cohn—he's a dancer. Bill Gorton—he's a professional Pokémon player. Mike—He's bankrupt and waiting to marry Brett. Brett Ashley—she's… well, she's Brett."

Pedro's English was surprisingly good, and he and Brett immediately fell into an intense conversation. I noticed Pedro kept glancing at the mirror, checking his appearance while talking to her.

Just then, Montoya entered the dining room. When he saw Pedro sitting at our table with a drink in his hand, laughing with Brett, his face went completely white. He looked at me with such betrayal and disappointment that I felt physically sick. His expression said everything: *How could you? You promised to protect the boy!*

Montoya shook his head slowly and walked away without a word.

Pedro eventually excused himself, but not before promising to meet Brett later for "Spanish lessons."

The moment Pedro left, Mike exploded on Cohn. I was amazed because for once I felt Cohn didn't deserve it but Mike had to take his jealousy and bankruptcy out on someone.

"You want a dance-off, you prancing freak?" Mike announced, jumping up onto a chair. "I'll show you some real moves!"

Mike proceeded to attempt moonwalks and backflips, crashing into tables and sending drinks flying. "You want a dance-off? I'll give you a dance-off!"

But suddenly, mid-backflip, Mike stopped and grabbed the back of a chair for support. I looked at his face and knew a new level of awkwardness was about to be unleashed.

"I LOVE HER, MAN!" he shouted, tears streaming down his face. "Can't you see I love her? She's all I've got!"

The entire dining room fell silent. Even the waiters stopped to stare at this grown man having a public breakdown.

"Okay," I said, standing up quickly. "Let's get out of here."

"Where are we going?" Mike asked, tears streaming down his cheeks.

"To the bar, of course!" Bill announced. "We just had drinks with dinner, now it's time for real drinks!"

"Oh boy," I muttered. "Why do I do this to myself?"

Mike seemed to instantly recover when he and Bill spotted some attractive local women and followed them to another bar.

Brett told Cohn he was being annoying and to get lost. Cohn walked slowly away, looking extremely dejected, turning his head back to us every few steps while Brett kept making a shooing gesture with her hands. Then she turned to me with that look I knew too well.

"Jake, darling, I want to do something I know I shouldn't."

"I know you want to see Pedro again," I said. "Let's not drag this out any further. This is a comedy, after all, not some endless tragedy."

We found Pedro back in the dining room, now alone, still occasionally glancing at the mirror.

"Pedro," I said seriously, "I warned you earlier. Are you absolutely sure about this? Because I'll warn you one more time—you don't know what you're getting into."

Pedro looked at himself in the mirror, ran a hand through his perfect hair, and smiled confidently.

"With these looks?" he said, half to me and half to his reflection. "I can handle anything."

I sighed and left them to their "Spanish lessons." As I walked away, I turned back to see them laughing together, Brett hanging on his every word, Pedro constantly checking his appearance in the mirror.

At a table in the corner, Montoya sat alone with his head in his hands, an empty bottle in front of him, and what appeared to be tears on the tablecloth.

The Supreme Roosters were coming tomorrow, Pedro was falling under Brett's curse, and I had a terrible feeling that everything was about to go very, very wrong.

Chapter 17: Cohninator and Supreme Roosters

I left Brett and Pedro to their "Spanish lessons" and went looking for Mike and Bill, following their usual trail of destruction through Pamplona's drinking establishments. It wasn't hard to track them—I just had to follow the sounds of chaos and the trail of empty bottles.

I found them outside the Gallo Borracho with two police officers who looked like they'd been having the most exhausting night of their careers.

"Listen, señores," one officer was saying in broken English, "I know it's fiesta, but you have a serious problem. How are you even still standing? Please, drink some water or something. Anything without alcohol."

"Water?" Mike said, horrified. "During fiesta? That's practically sacrilege!"

"We're fine, officer," Bill added, swaying dangerously. "We're just getting warmed up."

The policemen looked at each other in disbelief. One muttered something in Spanish that sounded like a prayer for strength. Mike and Bill were completely unfazed by the police presence and were actively flirting with a group of local women who had gathered to watch the spectacle. One particularly attractive woman with dark hair was laughing at Mike's attempts at Spanish.

"Her name's Lolita," Bill whispered to me conspiratorially. "Mike's completely smitten. Says she's his 'destiny' or some nonsense."

I grabbed Mike by the arm as he started to follow Lolita toward another bar.

"Mike, you need to listen to me!" I said urgently.

"What? Can't it wait? Lolita wants to show me the authentic local drinking customs."

"Mike, think about this. All the bad luck in your life—when did it start?"

Mike's drunken expression suddenly became more focused. "When I met Brett," he said slowly. "On the day I introduced her to my parents, my father died. Heart attack, right there at dinner. On the day we announced our engagement, my mother died—choked while eating yogurt. Then recently the market crash, the money simply vanished…"

"That's what I'm trying to tell you," I said. "She's cursed. I've confirmed it. Every man who gets involved with her—"

"He's right," Bill chimed in. "Look at Cohn—he's falling apart piece by piece. Count Cholesterol keeps having heart attacks. You went bankrupt. It's all connected."

Mike looked thoughtful for a moment, then glanced over at Lolita, who was motioning for him to join her.

"Well," Mike said with a grin, "I think the curse is a thing of the past! Who needs Brett when there are locals like this?"

He ran off into the bar, practically bouncing with newfound optimism. Bill and I shrugged to each other and then followed because, of course, we needed to drink more—we were expatriates in action, after all.

Inside the bar, we'd barely ordered our drinks when a commotion erupted near the entrance. The crowd parted, and there was Robert Cohn, wearing his "I Love Brett" sequined shirt that was now so tight it looked like it might cut off his circulation. But something was different—he had enormous metal braces on both legs that made him look like some kind of mechanical dancer.

"Listen, you two!" Cohn announced, pointing dramatically at Mike and me while posing with his other hand on his hip. "The reason Brett isn't with me is because you're both holding me back from my true potential! Now watch this!"

What happened next was, I have to admit, genuinely impressive. Cohn began an elaborate interpretive dance routine that combined elements of ballet, breakdancing, and what appeared to be some kind of martial arts. His leg braces gave him incredible height and stability, allowing him to perform moves that should have been impossible for someone with his injuries.

"Where the heck did he get those braces?" Bill whispered.

"More importantly," I said, "how is he suddenly so good at this?"

Cohn spun, leaped, and contorted through the air with surprising grace. He jumped from a bar table, soared over the still-unconscious Count Cholesterol (who was still slumped in a chair with his oxygen tank), and landed on another table in a dramatic pose that would have made any professional dancer jealous.

The crowd that had gathered was cheering him on. Local women were throwing flowers. A mariachi band appeared from nowhere and started playing accompaniment music.

"¡Increíble!" someone shouted.

"¡¿Es ese el americano raro?!" called another.

How was this possible? I kept thinking about the curse, but maybe it worked differently on different people. Maybe Cohn was channeling his obsession into actual talent. Or the curse was setting him up for something far worse.

After his final landing, Cohn faced Mike and me with a triumphant expression.

"Now that you are completely dominated by my perfect dancing," he declared, "admit that Brett belongs with me!"

Mike and I grabbed our drinks and said in unison, "Sure!" as we turned our backs to him.

"Don't you turn your backs on me!" Cohn shouted. "You aren't getting off that easy! Prepare to be mauled by the Cohninator!"

Cohn started throwing punches at me, but they were so weak they felt like a small child having a tantrum. I started laughing.

"Stop, Cohn, that tickles! What are you doing?"

He did the same thing to Mike with identical results—tiny, ineffective punches that wouldn't have hurt a butterfly.

"There!" Cohn said, breathing heavily from his exertion. "Now you'll let Brett and me live in peace!"

"Oh, Cohn," I said, wiping tears of laughter from my eyes, "there's something I should tell you."

"What is it?" Cohn said, sweaty with rage and effort.

"Brett's with Pedro."

"NOOOOOOOO!!!!" Cohn wailed, a sound so anguished that even the mariachi band stopped playing.

He ran off crying, pushing through the crowd and accidentally knocking over several tables in his panic. His leg braces made him move in lurches like a small Frankenstein having a tantrum.

"What a weirdo," said one of the spectators.

A little local kid tugged on his mother's dress. "Mommy, is that what an American is like?"

I looked over at Mike, who was already deep in conversation with Lolita, teaching her to play some drinking game that involved balancing beer bottles on your head. He seemed genuinely happy for the first time since I'd known him.

"Well, that was easy—maybe Mike will be all right," I said to Bill.

"Want to play darts?" Bill asked casually, as if nothing unusual had happened.

"Sure," I said. After all, we were used to Cohn being weird.

We spent the next hour playing darts and drinking, while Mike regaled Lolita with stories about his life before Brett. His whole demeanor had changed—he was confident, funny, charming. I could see the curse dissipating right before my eyes.

Eventually, I decided to head back to the hotel. As I approached the building, I could hear Cohn's voice echoing through the entire structure.

"JAKE! JAKE! I NEED TO TALK TO YOU!"

He was shouting from his room, but the sound carried all the way down to the lobby. The night clerk looked exhausted.

"Señor Cohn has been doing this for two hours," he said wearily. "We've had complaints from other guests, but he won't stop."

I apologized to the night clerk as I trudged upstairs and knocked on Cohn's door.

"Come in, Jake," came his muffled voice.

I entered to find Cohn sitting in the dark, clutching his Ratty Rat stuffed animal and still wearing his sequined shirt and leg braces.

"I want to apologize," he said dramatically, "for beating you up so badly."

I stared at him. "Uh… yeah. Okay. It's fine, Cohn. Just go to bed or something."

"You don't understand the depth of my regret," Cohn continued, hugging his Ratty tighter. "But don't worry. You'll see tomorrow… *oh yes, you'll all see tomorrow.*"

"What's that supposed to mean?"

"Nothing," Cohn said quickly. "Just… you'll see. Everyone will see what true courage looks like."

I brushed it off as another strange Cohn thing and left him to his Ratty Rat and his delusions.

I woke up late the next morning to the sound of rockets and screaming. Today was the running of the Supreme Roosters, and from the sounds outside, it was already well underway. I threw on my clothes and rushed to the nearest viewing area.

The crowds of people had already filled up the balconies and best viewing spots. All I could find was a place to squeeze up against a fence but I could barely see through the wooden planks. What I witnessed was the most horrific running in fiesta history.

The Supreme Roosters were nothing like regular fighting birds. Through gaps in the fence, I caught flashes of enormous black shapes moving with supernatural speed. These creatures were easily twice the size of normal roosters, with blood-red eyes and beaks sharpened to surgical points. They moved like shadows, coordinating their attacks with military precision.

The runners had discovered early that these were no ordinary birds. Through the planks, I saw flashes of terror-stricken faces, clouds of dust, and brief glimpses of the black death-machines pursuing the fleeing crowd. The smell of fear mixed with the overwhelming odor of what can only be described as a giant, murderous hen house.

The screaming was unlike anything I'd ever heard. These weren't the excited shouts of traditional running—these were screams of genuine terror and mortal danger.

Eventually, a rocket went off with a sound that resembled a "Cock-a-doodle-doo," signaling that all the roosters had made it to the fighting corral. But something was wrong. The usual cheers and celebration that followed a successful run were replaced by an eerie silence broken only by the sound of ambulance bells.

I worked my way through the dispersing crowd and learned the horrible truth: no runners had survived. The Supreme Roosters had killed everyone in their path. A quarter of the town had been running. A quarter of the town was now gone forever.

I did the only natural thing you do in this book—I went to get a drink at the café and wait for my friends.

The waiter who served me looked shell-shocked. "I've worked fiestas for thirty years," he said, his hands shaking as he poured my coffee. "I've never seen anything like this. Why? Why Supreme Roosters? What was wrong with regular roosters? All for fun… badly cogido." He shook his head. "All for entertainment."

I saw Montoya walk past the café window. Our eyes met through the glass, and he gave me another look of such disappointment and betrayal that I felt sick. He kept walking, slowly shaking his head.

Later, back at the hotel, Bill and Mike found me in the bar. They were completely unphased from the rooster carnage—probably due to the number of drinks they've already had today. What was more interesting to them is what had happened with Cohn, Pedro, and Brett. The waiter brought us each another drink as they proceeded to fill me in on the part of the Cohn story that I'd missed.

"You should have seen it," Bill said, barely containing his laughter. "Cohn found Pedro and Brett and challenged him to a dance-off."

"A dance-off?" I asked. "Where did this happen?"

"Right in the middle of the street," Bill said. "Cohn was probably stalking them, and you know how he needs to have a crowd when he dances. I'm just surprised Pedro accepted and how long it went on for."

"How long was it?" I asked.

"Eight hours," Mike added, grinning widely. "Eight straight hours of competitive interpretive dance. Pedro accepted the challenge, and apparently he's quite good himself."

"They went challenge for challenge," Bill continued. "Cohn would do some elaborate routine about 'the anguish of unrequited love,' and Pedro would respond with something about 'the glory of the rooster fight.' The crowd kept growing. People were placing bets."

"Pedro might have pulled a hamstring," Mike said. "Or maybe a groin muscle. Either way, he's going to be exhausted for tomorrow's Supreme Rooster fights."

"Why did it take Brett eight hours to tell Cohn to get lost?" I asked.

"She was passed out for most of it," Bill explained. "Apparently, she'd been drinking with Pedro before the dance-off started."

We sat in silence. I was amazed at the events of the day and was trying to process it all. After about two minutes Mike suggested we play pool.

Despite the mass carnage, Mike was in incredibly good spirits. He'd spent most of the day with Lolita, who apparently ran a successful vineyard and had been teaching him about wine investment opportunities.

"The best part," Mike said, after winning his third game in a row, "is that her father wants to go into business with me. Something about importing Spanish wines to England. My luck's completely turned around!"

"It's the end of the curse," I said.

"What curse?" Mike asked, then laughed. "Oh, right. That old thing. That's history now."

But as we drank and talked, I couldn't shake a feeling of dread about tomorrow's rooster fights. Pedro was injured and exhausted from dancing for eight hours. The Supreme Roosters had just proven they were killing machines. And Cohn's ominous words from the night before kept echoing in my mind: "You'll see tomorrow… everyone will see what true courage looks like."

Whatever was coming, I had the terrible feeling that things were about to get much worse before they got better.

Chapter 18: Roosters Reign and Heroes Fall

At noon Bill and I were at the café. It was crowded with tourists, locals, and what appeared to be several people who looked like they'd survived a war. Of course, considering that a quarter of the town had been killed by Supreme Roosters the day before, they had survived a war.

The town was still crowded despite the carnage. Every street was full of people who seemed determined to pretend that mass poultry-related death was just part of the authentic Spanish experience. Big motor-cars from Biarritz and San Sebastian kept driving up and parking around the square, bringing fresh tourists who had no idea what they were walking into.

"Look at that," Bill said, pointing to a sight-seeing car packed with tourists. "They're all taking pictures of the bloodstains."

The parades through the streets continued; the fiesta must go on. The dancers were all quite drunk, which wasn't unusual, but today they seemed to be drinking with the desperate intensity of people who might not live to see tomorrow. It was the last day of the fiesta, and everyone was acting like it might literally be the last day of their lives.

The fiesta crowd was solid and unbroken, but the tourist cars made little islands of horrified onlookers. When the cars emptied, you could spot the tourists easily—they were the ones asking waiters things like "Is it normal for roosters to kill that many people?" and "Should we have gotten travel insurance that covers poultry attacks?" It was like a new batch of soldiers arriving at the front lines. Their clothes were unstained and wrinkle-free. Their souls unburdened from the images of the past.

The street was constantly full of music, but it had a frantic quality today. The drums kept pounding and the pipes were going, but underneath it all you could hear the occasional distant crow of the Supreme Roosters in their corral, a sound that made everyone's blood run cold.

Inside the cafés, men and women were gripping their tables and each other's shoulders, singing and swaying together, but their knuckles were white and their voices cracked with fear.

"Here comes Brett," Bill said.

I looked and saw her coming through the crowd in the square, walking with her head up, as though the fiesta were being staged in her honor and mass death was just part of the entertainment. She looked radiant, completely unaffected by the fact that her presence had turned a traditional festival into a supernatural horror show.

"Hello, you chaps!" she said. "I say, I have a thirst. All this tragedy makes one rather parched."

"Get another big beer," Bill said to the waiter.

"Where's Mike?" Brett asked, looking around.

I exchanged glances with Bill. "Oh, he said he had a headache and needed a nap," I said carefully. "Yep, he's definitely not having the time of his life with his new soul mate."

"Hmm," Brett said suspiciously. "Mike never would pass up an opportunity to drink, even if he was on his deathbed. Which, given recent events, might be more literal than usual."

"How's Pedro?" I asked, trying to change the subject.

"He's fine," Brett said, but I noticed her hand shake slightly as she lifted her beer. "If it wasn't for that annoying Robert, we would have had a wonderful time. Instead, I spent eight hours watching two grown men act like children in a dance competition."

"Speaking of Cohn," Bill said, "has anyone seen him around?"

"No," I said, remembering his ominous words from the night before. "But he was saying something strange yesterday about 'true courage' and 'you'll see tomorrow.'"

Brett shrugged. "Typical Robert nonsense. He probably means he's going to perform another interpretive dance about his feelings."

After lunch, Brett announced she wanted to go to church to pray for Pedro.

"Don't you remember what happened last time?" I asked. "You almost burst into flames."

"Oh, I'll be fine," Brett said dismissively. "Lightning never strikes twice."

"Ok," I said, "but I warned you."

The three of us made our way to the chapel. The moment Brett stepped inside, beads of sweat appeared on her forehead. We took a seat in one of the pews and bowed our heads.

"You know," I whispered, "it doesn't have to be that hard. You're praying, not weightlifting."

I could hear her prayer, and it wasn't what you'd expect: "Please, God, let Pedro never lose his looks, and let his pants always look amazing. And maybe let him survive today, but mostly the pants thing."

After about a minute, I swear I saw smoke wafting up from her hair.

"Okay!" Brett said suddenly, jumping up. "We should be good now."

We went back to the hotel café, where we saw Montoya, who stared at us with the blankest, most disappointed expression in human history. It was the look of a man watching his life's work being destroyed by supernatural forces beyond his control. We put our heads down and sped up walking to avoid him.

"I should check on Mike," Brett said.

"I don't think that's such a great idea," Bill said quickly. "I'm sure he's sleeping it off."

We opened the door to Mike's room. There was the shape of something in the bed. I could tell the pillows were arranged under the blankets to make it look like someone was sleeping.

"See?" I said, closing the door quickly. "He's sleeping just fine. Let's let him rest."

Brett seemed suspicious but let it go.

We went back downstairs to the café. As we sat in the café, you could feel the electric buzz of anticipation for the afternoon's Supreme Rooster fights. People were carrying signs and posters of their favorite roosters. These birds were so vicious they had developed their own fan base.

Some people had signs reading "Chicken Supreme," and it was confusing because you couldn't tell if they were fans or actually selling a dish called Chicken Supreme. One vendor was shouting, "Get your Chicken Supreme! The only Supreme that won't kill you!"

The fiesta boiled over toward the rooster arena, and we went with the crowd. The place was packed beyond capacity. The President was there, flags were flying high, and despite all the rain, the weather was perfect—calm, with firm ground. Perfect weather for rooster fighting, if you ignored the fact that these particular roosters were supernatural killing machines.

For the last day of the fiesta, three legendary rooster fighters had been brought in: Belmonte, known as "The Chicken Whisperer" for his ability to calm the birds; Marcial, nicknamed "Egg Beater" for his ruthless killing techniques; and Camacho, called "Macho Camacho" because he fought shirtless, his muscles rippling in the sunlight.

And then there was Pedro Romero, already becoming known as "Pedro the Kid" or simply "The Legend." At only nineteen, there was no one better, and there never would be.

The arena filled with the pageantry of rooster fighting tradition. First came the ceremonial hens, circling the arena while mariachi music played. Then came the egg basket holders—each matador had a custom basket, and if their holders found an egg laid by one of the hens, it signified good luck.

No such eggs were found that day.

Next came the sword handlers with weapons for each matador, followed by the cape bearers. Each matador's cape was covered in sponsor logos—The Count's Heart-Stoppin' Chicken was prominently displayed on all of their capes. Evidently, the Count was hedging his bets by sponsoring everyone.

I looked through my binoculars at Pedro and thought I saw him limping.

"Do you see what you did?" I said to Brett. "He's already limping."

"Hey," Brett protested, "that was Robert's fault, not mine."

The music started, and the matadors came in procession, walking once around the arena and stopping in front of the President's box. They bowed, and the crowd roared.

Before the fighting officially began, the matadors would present their special capes to those they wished to dedicate their performance to. The other matadors gave their capes to friends or sponsors.

Don't do it, Pedro, I thought desperately. *Don't seal your fate.*

But Pedro took off his cape and handed it to his sword handler, who made his way through the crowd to Brett and presented it to her with a flourish.

"Oh, how lovely!" Brett said, examining the cape. "The fabric is exquisite."

I put my head in my hands.

Belmonte was up first. He was clearly older, slower, and although he'd once been a great rooster fighter, he was well past his prime.

"This guy shouldn't be here," I told Brett and Bill. "Look at him. He should be retired, sitting on a porch somewhere, telling stories about the old days."

The arena's electronic scoreboard lit up: "MATADORS: 0, ROOSTERS: 0"

Below that, a timer showed: "ROOSTER RELEASE: UNO... DOS... TRES"

"Watch the timer," I reminded Bill and Brett. "Every thirty seconds a rooster is released until there are three roosters against the matador. The crowd will yell, 'UNO!', 'DOS!', 'TRES!'"

The Chicken Whisperer entered the ring. He took his place in the center of the arena and drew his sword.

"UNO!"

The first Supreme Rooster bolted out of its cage. This was the first time many of us were able to get a clean look at a Supreme Rooster. The beast was impressive. All black with red eyes, strutting as if it owned the arena. Confident in itself—aware of its power. It looked around at the crowd. It slowly kicked up dust with its feet as if getting ready for battle. Its eyes narrowed when it saw spectators with chicken tacos.

Belmonte immediately began talking to the first rooster in soothing tones. Through my binoculars, I could see him discretely dropping chicken feed down through his pants leg. The rooster was calmed by Belmonte's voice and feeding technique.

"That's how he did it all these years," I said. "He's just been bribing them with food!"

"DOS!"

The second rooster looked aggressive at first but after some food appeared manageable.

The crowd started jeering. "Fight! Fight! We want blood!"

"TRES!"

The third rooster emerged, and this one was different. This was clearly the leader—larger, more intelligent, with eyes that seemed to glow with malevolent purpose. He stared at Belmonte until Belmonte was forced to look away.

"He lost the staring contest, mommy," I heard a kid with a Belmonte t-shirt on say.

Uh-oh, I thought.

The lead rooster let out a series of strategic squawks, organizing his companions. They split up, distracting Belmonte while the leader circled behind him. The old matador lost sight of the third rooster, who rushed up behind him and delivered a flying, twisting, spear-like lunge that would have made a ninja proud. The rooster, twisting like a cyclone, flew right through his back and out the front of his chest.

The Chicken Whisperer was no more.

Mariachi music started playing as they removed the body. The PA announcer's voice crackled over the speakers: "Everything is normal, folks! This is completely normal! Nothing to see here!"

Down the aisle in the stands, a concession seller was yelling, "Cotton candy! Peanuts! Trauma counseling!"

Bill ordered some peanuts and shrugged at me. "Hey, this makes me hungry."

Brett was completely unphased and was looking around for a drink vendor. "Where does one get alcohol in this place?"

I looked at the kid with the Belmonte shirt. He now had a flag that read, "Marcial: The Egg Beater."

"Marcial can do it, right daddy," he said. His parents nodded nervously.

I looked across the arena and saw Montoya in the corner, still just staring at me with pure disappointment. I swallowed nervously.

Marcial was second. After seeing what the roosters had done to Belmonte, the "Egg Beater" looked focused and serious. He stood there sharpening his sword, waiting.

"UNO!"

The first rooster came out bobbing and weaving like a professional boxer. Marcial didn't try to toy with it but went on a direct attack with his sword. He chased it around the arena, his sword flashing in the sunlight, but he couldn't land a hit. He was swinging wildly and only managed to damage the sponsorship signs draped along the fence of the arena. Of course, the biggest one was from The Count's Heart-Stoppin' Chicken with a new slogan: 'Chicken You Can *Count* On!'

"DOS!"

The second rooster emerged, moving with supernatural speed. Marcial's sword swinging attacks become wilder. He was now just spinning around hoping to hit anything.

"TRES!"

The lead rooster entered and just stared Marcial down with those glowing red eyes. This rooster gave a squawk and the other roosters stopped where they were. All the roosters were standing like statues while Marcial was still swinging his sword like a blind mad man. It was hard to hear but I swear I heard the roosters laughing.

After another thirty minutes of Marcial getting in some serious cardio he ran out of steam. He couldn't even hold his sword up and just stood there with his head down, sweat profusely dripping from his face.

"Marcial's still got it. Let's cheer for him!" the kid next to us said as he tried to get a wave started.

The leader gave another commanding squawk, and all three roosters rushed Marcial simultaneously with speed I'd never seen before. It was like watching a coordinated military assault, if the military were comprised entirely of murderous poultry.

The poor guy didn't stand a chance. Mariachi music started up again as they removed another body. The PA announcer came back on over the speakers: "Hope everyone is enjoying the fights! Belmonte and Marcial merchandise now half-off at the concession stands!"

I looked over at the kid next to us, he now had a Macho Camacho hat that read, "Who Needs Shirts When You're Macho Like Camacho."

Scoreboard update: "ROOSTERS: 2, MATADORS: 0"

"Beer! Ice cold beer here!" called the concession guy.

Bill and Brett partook. Montoya continued staring. I looked away.

Camacho was third. He entered the ring without a shirt, clearly doused in baby oil, his muscles glistening as he strutted around the arena like he was on a magazine cover. He started posing while walking to every corner of the arena, really playing it up for the crowd.

"He is quite the showman," Bill said.

"UNO!"

Camacho decided that he would prove how macho he was by catching the roosters with his bare hands, it was his signature move. He lunged repeatedly at the first rooster but couldn't catch it. Every time he missed he'd flex for the crowd.

"DOS!"

Now there were two roosters just toying with him, making him chase them in circles. Camacho, still not fully appreciating the danger, continued flexing around the arena. At one point, he held up his hand to the roosters who stopped plotting their attack and stood looking confused. One of Camacho's staff jumped over the arena fence and doused him with more baby oil. Once appropriately glistening he motioned to the roosters to continue.

"TRES!"

The leader came out, and Camacho, in a moment of either incredible bravery or incredible stupidity, threw his sword to the corner.

"Fight me like a man!" he shouted at the rooster.

"But it's a rooster," Bill pointed out.

The lead rooster held out his wing and beckoned him to fight with a flip of his wing that said, "Come here." Camacho gritted his teeth and lunged at the leader. Unfortunately, his staff forgot to check to see if his shoes were tied. Camacho tripped over his own feet. That's when the roosters saw their advantage and pounced with surgical precision.

Macho Camacho was now the third victim of the day.

More Mariachi music played as the removal crew came back on. I looked over at the kid next to us. His parents were counting the money they still had before buying a huge foam finger for him that read, "Pedo's #1."

"I don't like this," I said to Brett. "Let's tell Pedro to call this off."

"What do you mean?" she said, not looking away from her binoculars, which were focused on Pedro's posterior region.

"Brett, three men just died horribly."

"Oh, they died?" she said absently. "That's unfortunate. But look at how those pants fit!"

I shook my head in disbelief and made my way around to where Pedro was standing during the intermission.

"Pedro," I said urgently, "you need to call this off. Those roosters aren't normal. They're killing machines."

Pedro looked at me with that confident smile. "Those other guys were sloppy, past their prime. They shouldn't even have been here. Go back and sit down and watch how a master handles these birds."

He pulled out a pocket mirror and checked his hair.

I gave up and went back to my seat.

Then it was Pedro's turn. The main event.

Pedro took center stage of the arena, checking his equipment with a serious expression on his face. Then he pulled out his pocket mirror again and checked his hair.

"Wow, he's gorgeous," Brett sighed.

"UNO!"

The first Supreme Rooster bolted out, confident and sure of its supremacy. You could see it in the rooster's cocky attitude—it strutted around like it owned the place.

But unlike the previous fights, this time it looked like the matador was in control. Pedro was playing with the rooster, dodging its attacks with graceful ease, controlling its movements without the bird even realizing it.

"DOS!"

The second rooster emerged. Now it was two against one, but Pedro was still dominating every move. The roosters tried their coordinated tactics, but Pedro anticipated everything.

The crowd went wild. "Pedro the Kid! Pedro the Kid!"

T-shirt vendors appeared from nowhere, hawking Pedro merchandise. "Get your Pedro shirts! Pedro hats! Pedro action figures!"

Maybe I was wrong, I thought. *He looks amazing out there.*

I looked at the kid with the big foam finger next to us. He finally looked happy, waving his finger all over, hitting the heads of everyone around him.

"TRES!"

The leader bolted out and stopped, assessing the situation. It did a series of strategic squawks, and different attack patterns took place, but Pedro fended them all off and then went on the offensive.

Pedro's performance was incredible! The crowd was going absolutely wild. I caught Montoya's eye from across the arena, and he gave me a solid thumbs up and nodded approvingly.

It looked like everything would be okay.

But then something happened.

Pedro was fighting directly below where Brett and I were sitting, and he looked up. He looked up at Brett with those dark, beautiful eyes.

Right then, I could tell something had changed. Pedro started limping again, his concentration broken.

"See!" I said, tapping Brett on the arm. "Do you see? He pulled his hamstring!"

"Oh, he's fine," Brett said, never lowering her binoculars from his pants region. "Just look at those magnificent pants."

"He's not fine!" I said. "How can you fight Supreme Roosters with a pulled hammy?"

As if the limping weren't bad enough, Pedro fended off the roosters and then, in the moment when he should have regrouped, he pulled out his pocket mirror to check his looks and hair again.

As he was admiring himself in the mirror, a loud, piercing squawk filled the arena. Flying like a rocket, the lead rooster tore through the mirror in Pedro's hand, shattering it and slicing his palm in the same motion.

Immediately after that, one of the other roosters pecked his left Achilles tendon. Pedro fell to one knee, looking around as he dropped his sword.

And then, the third rooster pecked his right Achilles tendon.

I caught Montoya's eye again. His mouth was gaping open, and he was shaking his head in profound disappointment.

Pedro, now on both knees, was at the mercy of the three killers. The leader stepped up to finish the job when, out of nowhere, seemingly like Iron Man, a figure dropped right into the middle of the arena, kicking up a huge cloud of dust.

When the dust settled, there were two figures in the arena with the roosters: Pedro… and… Cohn!?

Cohn stood tall and then pointed dramatically at Brett and then made that annoying heart symbol with his hands.

"Cohn!" I yelled. "What are you doing in there? Get out of there!"

Bill was shouting, "What's wrong with you? You can't dance your way out of this!"

Or could he?

Looking at Cohn, he was now like a mechanical figure from a steampunk fantasy. His legs now had enormous mechanical contraptions attached to them—pistons, gears, and steam vents that hissed and whirred with each movement. He made a twirling gesture, flung out his hand, and a flaming sword materialized from thin air.

The crowd was in awe. I was in awe. This was actually amazing.

But not only did he look cool for once, he was moving like I'd never seen him move—jumping twenty feet in the air, flipping, somersaulting, not a trace of Beige Poupon anywhere. His interpretive dance training had somehow merged with advanced robotics to create the ultimate fighting machine.

He was protecting Pedro, deflecting rooster attacks with balletic grace while his mechanical legs provided impossible speed and agility.

But after a while, you could tell the old Cohn was coming back because he started looking toward Brett after each impressive move.

"See who's a real man now!" he yelled to her between backflips.

"I'm authentic!" he shouted while deflecting a rooster attack.

"Peak masculinity!" he announced while doing a perfect pirouette.

"And I have better pants than Pedro!"

While he was showboating for Brett, the lead rooster made an incredibly sophisticated attack. Cohn dodged it, but I saw what looked like a piston explode from the mechanical contraption on his left leg. Steam hissed out, and pieces of metal started falling all over the arena.

Pedro started laughing despite his injuries.

Soon, more mechanical parts were failing. Gears ground to a halt, pistons seized up, and steam poured from multiple ruptures. Cohn was rapidly transforming back to his normal, pathetic human self, barely able to walk with all his ACL issues.

He tried to jump and managed to get maybe half an inch off the ground.

Eventually, he found himself next to Pedro, both of them on their knees in the center of the arena. They looked at each other and, in a moment of surprising humanity, held hands.

The arena was dead silent except for one voice: "POPCORN! GET YOUR POPCORN HERE!"

Then, after a series of strategic squawks from the leader, the final attack came. It was too fast for human eyes to follow—just a flash of black feathers, razor-sharp beaks, and swirling dust.

When it was over, Cohn and Pedro were lying motionless in the center of the arena. The roosters stood over them, each with one leg on the backs of the fallen, posing for the cameras. It was dead silent in the arena.

"CRACKER JACKS!" called the vendor.

I looked at Montoya across the arena. He looked up at me and made a throat-cutting gesture. He was no longer disappointed—it was pure hatred now.

Brett looked up from her binoculars and said, "Hey, what's going on? The pants aren't moving."

She had been completely oblivious to the carnage because she'd been zoomed in on Pedro's outfit the entire time.

She surveyed the scene. "Oh, poop!" she said.

"Yeah, 'oh poop' is right," I said. "Don't you see what you've done? Now you've gotten Cohn *and* Pedro killed."

"Me?" she said indignantly. "It was the roosters, not me! Oh well, maybe we should get a drink."

The mariachi music started up again, and the PA announcer thanked everyone for their attendance and said they looked forward to seeing us at next year's fiesta. Also, all merchandise was 75% off!

The final score flashed on the electronic board: "ROOSTERS: 4, MATADORS + COHN: 0"

I looked at the kid who was taking off his big foam finger and said, "You know Spain is really good at Fútbol, you should give that a shot."

We were all exhausted after the fight, and now we had to fight our way through the crowd to get back to the hotel. It was the last day of the fiesta, and Bill and Brett still wanted to drink.

"How can your stomachs keep this up?" I asked. "Also, people died out there! Cohn died! Pedro died! And the first thing you can think of is alcohol?"

"Yes," Brett said cheerfully. "It's a start."

We found our way to the café, and within minutes Brett had walked away. I saw her talking to Count Cholesterol, who had somehow survived his multiple heart attacks and business failures. He seemed to be on the rebound but now Brett was hovering over him, checking the size of his wallet.

"Hey," Bill said, "let's go check on Mike."

I walked over to say goodbye to Brett and the Count, then we went up to Mike's room. We found him there playing cards with Lolita, both of them laughing and looking genuinely happy.

Bill and I filled them in on all the events.

Mike was blown away. "Cohn's really dead?"

"Very dead," I confirmed.

"Well," Mike said thoughtfully, "I'm kind of sorry about it, but he did it to himself. He didn't respect the curse."

"What curse?" Lolita asked.

"Long story," I said. "Let's go down and get something to eat and we can fill you in."

When we made it to the dining room, there was no sign of Brett at all. One of the waiters approached me.

"The English lady wanted me to tell you she is going to Madrid with the Count. She left on the seven o'clock train."

"Thank you," I said.

When we sat down, I told Mike, Bill, and Lolita the news. We looked at each other, then at the empty chairs where Cohn and Brett would usually sit.

And you know what? We had one of the best nights of our lives.

Book III: The Tab Closes

Chapter 19: Peace Found and Peace Interrupted

In the morning it was all over. The fiesta was finished. Amid all the carnage and supernatural poultry attacks, the city began the monumental task of cleaning itself up. Empty buckets of the Count's twelve-piece meal were littered throughout the streets. Buses were running nonstop, evacuating traumatized tourists who kept asking questions like "Is this normal for Spanish festivals?" and "Should we write reviews warning other people?"

I found my way downstairs to an outside café where I could finally enjoy some peace and quiet. The waiters weren't rushing around frantically—they were moving slowly, like people recovering from a natural disaster. Everyone was laid back, trying to process what they'd just survived.

For the first time in weeks, I was drinking water and having a healthy breakfast. Real eggs, no Beige Poupon in sight. It felt revolutionary.

Bill came over, looking like he'd aged five years in the past week.

"Well," he said, sitting down heavily, "it's over."

"Thank the Lord," I said.

"I'm glad you invited me, but I don't think I'd come to this festival again. Ever. Not even if someone paid me."

"Well," I said, "I don't think I will either, because I'll never be able to stay at Montoya's again. In fact, we better get out of here before he finds me and makes me pay for Pedro's funeral expenses."

Mike joined us, and he looked completely different—he looked 5 years younger. He was relaxed, happy, and practically glowing. He was carrying what appeared to be a telegram and grinning from ear to ear.

"Where are you all headed?" I asked as we finished breakfast.

"I'm going to Paris," Bill said. "Back to civilization, where roosters are just normal-sized and non-murderous."

"I'm taking Lolita to England to meet my family!" Mike announced proudly. "And I just got this telegram—one of my investments came through! I'm rich again!"

He waved the telegram excitedly. "Apparently, when you're not cursed, your financial decisions start making sense. Who knew?"

They both looked at me expectantly.

"I'm going to San Sebastian," I said.

They exchanged knowing glances. "Oh, because Beth is there?" Bill asked with a grin.

"Well, maybe," I said, trying to play it cool. "But the beach is also nice there, and we might run into each other. Accidentally. While I happen to be walking by her hotel. Repeatedly."

We said our goodbyes at the train station. Bill was practically running toward his train, muttering things like "Never again" and "I'm sticking to nice, safe places like war zones."

Mike shook my hand warmly. "Thanks for everything, Jake. Especially for helping me realize I was cursed. Best thing that ever happened to me, getting away from Brett."

"Take care of yourself, Mike. And congratulations on the investment."

"Cheers!"

The train to San Sebastian was like entering a different world. As we pulled away from Pamplona, I could feel my shoulders relaxing. No more interpretive dance emergencies. No more drama. No more supernatural poultry attacks. No vague famous mouse references. Just quiet countryside rolling by outside the window.

When I arrived in San Sebastian, the contrast was immediate. Everything was peaceful, clean, and mercifully free of aggressive roosters. I checked into a fancy hotel—the staff was friendly, the weather was perfect, and nobody was bleeding or having heart attacks in the lobby.

I planned to stay at least a week. Maybe longer if Beth was available.

I spent the first day at the beach, and it was exactly what I needed. The water was cool and refreshing and the weather was just the right temperature. I dove into the waves and felt the saltwater wash away weeks of accumulated stress.

I found a good spot on the warm sand and just lay there, letting the sun bake the anxiety out of my bones. At one point, I floated on my back in the calm water, staring up at the cloudless sky, and realized I couldn't remember the last time I'd felt this peaceful.

This was what normal life must be like.

The next day, I was having coffee at a beachside café when I saw a familiar figure walking along the promenade—it was Beth. She was wearing a simple white dress and carrying a Bible, looking like everything Brett wasn't—calm, genuine, and completely uninterested in causing chaos.

"Jake!" she called, waving. "I thought that might be you."

We stood there for a while catching each other up on all that had happened over a short period of time. She then took me to a nice local church where we listened to a sermon about what real purpose was in a lost world. After that we spent a wonderful day together at the beach, talking about books, travel, her work with orphanages—actual conversation instead of complaints about not meeting enough millionaires or discussions of cartoon characters. We swam together and sunbathed at the beach.

As we sat on the beach watching the sunset, I realized I was actually laughing. Not the nervous laughter that came from watching someone's interpretive dance disasters, but genuine, relaxed laughter.

"This is nice," Beth said simply.

"It really is," I agreed, and meant it.

On the third day, Beth suggested we take a trip to Trout Land, which was only a short train ride away.

"Sure, let's go. They have a great fishing lake," I said, remembering how much fun I had there with Bill and Harvey.

"I've heard it's actually quite *amusing*, do you get it?" she said. "Plus, how often do you get to visit a fish-themed amusement park?"

She had a point.

Trout Land was everything my friends weren't—clean fun and genuinely entertaining. We rode the Salmon Run roller coaster, ate trout-shaped cotton candy, and laughed at the ridiculousness of it all. Beth didn't try to turn it into some deep artistic statement or complain about the lack of eligible bachelors among the staff.

At one of the carnival games—a ring toss where you had to throw ping-pong balls into the mouths of mechanical trout that opened and closed randomly—I managed an impossible shot, banking the ball off the table and into a trout's mouth just as it snapped shut.

"WINNER! WINNER!" the game operator shouted.

I won Beth a large stuffed trout, which she hugged delightedly.

"My hero," she said, as she linked her arm with mine.

We spent the evening walking along the beach, and I found myself thinking that maybe, just maybe, I'd found someone who could make me forget about Brett and her destructive chaos entirely.

But the next morning at breakfast, the peace was shattered.

A telegram arrived, and the hotel concierge brought it over with an apologetic expression, as if he knew he was delivering bad news.

I opened it with growing dread:

COME TO HOTEL END OF THE LINE IN MADRID. IN BIG TROUBLE. COUNT IS DEAD. BRETT.

"Oh, boy," I said out loud. "Here we go again."

Beth looked up from her coffee. "Bad news?"

I showed her the telegram.

"Was she always like this?" I asked.

"Yes," Beth said simply. "That's why I'm afraid to be around her too much. She's my sister, and I love her, but…"

"So, you know about the curse?"

"Of course, I know about the curse. It's been like that ever since I can remember. I'm not sure how it started or what she needs to do to break it. Maybe there isn't a way."

She read the telegram again and continued, "And who is the count? He's dead?"

"Oh, it's a long story, but I bet she's just being dramatic. She probably means he's bankrupt or something."

Just then, another telegram arrived. This one was from England.

"How do all these people know exactly where I am?" I muttered, opening it:

Jake old boy! Lolita and I are engaged! Big wedding planned for next month in London. You must come! Bring a date! All the best. -Mike

"Hey, that's great," I said, my mood brightening slightly.

"What is it?" Beth asked.

"Mike is getting married to Lolita. I think he's safe from the curse for good."

"That's wonderful news!" Beth said genuinely.

"He invited me to the wedding. It's in London next month, and he said I could bring a date."

I looked at Beth and took her hand. "Will you be my plus-one?" I asked, hoping I didn't sound too eager.

"Of course," she said with a smile that made my heart skip.

I sighed and looked at Brett's telegram again. "Well, I have to go help your sister, I guess. But this is the last time. I mean it. After this, I'm done with Brett emergencies."

Beth reached into her purse and pulled out a piece of paper. "Here's the number where you can reach me when you get back to Paris."

I held the paper like it was made of gold.

"I'll call you the minute I get back," I promised.

Beth kissed me goodbye at the train station—a real kiss, not the air-kiss nonsense Brett specialized in—and I boarded the train to Madrid with mixed feelings. I was disappointed my vacation was cut short, but excited about the future with Beth.

I arrived at the Hotel End of the Line in Madrid, which turned out to be a surprisingly nice establishment. Of course, Brett hadn't bothered to mention a room number or any other useful information, so I went to the front desk.

"I'm looking for an English woman who checked in with Count Cholesterol," I told the concierge.

"Who?" she asked, looking confused.

"An English woman. With a rather large gentleman—smells like chicken, any of that ring a bell?"

"Oh yes, the English woman," she said, recognition dawning. She turned and called to someone inside. "There's *another* man looking for the English woman. Does she want to see this *other* man?"

Another man? I thought, then stopped myself. Of course there was another man. This was Brett.

Finally, the answer came back: yes, the English woman would see me.

I followed a maid down a long, dark corridor to what appeared to be the Presidential Suite. The smell of old fried chicken grew stronger with each step, which should have been my first warning.

The maid knocked on the door and quickly left, as if she couldn't get away fast enough.

"Jake, is that you?" came a shaky voice from inside.

"Yes, it's me."

She opened the door, and I was hit with a wall of smell and chaos. The room was a complete disaster—clothes everywhere, empty wine bottles scattered across every surface, food containers stacked like a hoarder's paradise. It looked like someone had been living there for twenty years, not five days.

"What the…!" I exclaimed. "What's the matter with you? Can't you at least pick up your things?"

"Why would I do that if I have a maid?" Brett said, as if this was perfectly reasonable.

"Well, what happened to your maid?"

"She won't come in because of that," Brett said, pointing casually toward the corner of the room.

In the corner sat Count Cholesterol, very obviously dead, slumped in an armchair with a twelve-piece bucket of The Count's Heart-Stoppin' Chicken on his lap. The soaked in grease had made the face on the bucket look like it was frowning. He looked peaceful, at least.

"WHAT?!" I shouted. "You didn't even tell anyone he was dead?"

"I was too embarrassed," Brett said. "And I thought I'd have to pay extra for the room."

I stared at her in disbelief. "Brett, there's a dead body in your hotel room."

"I know. It's been rather inconvenient. But what about the room charges? You'll pay for the room, right, Jakey boy?"

I felt my blood pressure rising but kept my cool. Through gritted teeth, I said, "Yes, *darling*, now let's go."

I was about to explode when we got to the front desk. I asked about the charges on the room and the concierge informed us that the room was already covered by Count Cholesterol's credit card, which had been set up for automatic payment.

"WHAT?!" I said. "So, this whole time, all you had to do was leave, or at least ask about the room?"

Brett just shrugged.

"Oh, by the way," I told the concierge as we headed for the door, "there's a huge dead guy in the Presidential Suite. You might want to… handle that."

The concierge looked confused, but we didn't wait around for questions.

"I need a drink," Brett announced the moment we hit the street.

"Of course you do," I said.

We found a very nice bar and ordered drinks. I ordered iced tea (unsweetened) and Brett ordered a whiskey sour. It was a classy place with actual glassware and bartenders who knew how to make proper cocktails.

"You're buying, right?" Brett asked as the drinks arrived.

I stared at her expressionlessly. "Yes. I've got it."

"And why are you getting iced tea? Are you feeling ok?"

"Yes, in fact I'm drinking iced tea precisely because I'm feeling ok," I replied.

I drank my drink faster than I normally would, anxious to get this over with and get back to Beth. Back to sanity.

"Wow, why are you drinking so fast?" Brett asked.

"No real reason," I said. "Just anxious to get back home. It's been a long holiday."

We agreed to take a taxi to the train station. As Madrid rolled by outside the windows, Brett seemed to be thinking.

"I think I'll go back to Mike," she said finally. "He's a pretty good guy after all, and I heard his investment portfolio is looking better."

"I'm not sure that's going to work," I said carefully.

"Why not?"

"Well, he's sort of... engaged to someone else at the moment."

"ENGAGED?!" Brett practically shrieked. "How did that happen?"

"Well, you know, those things just happen when you're not cursed anymore."

Brett was quiet for a moment, then I saw that look creep into her eyes—the calculating look that meant she was about to cause more chaos.

"Well," she said, turning to me with a coy smile, "you know, I think I've been getting better about my foot fungus repulsion. I might be able to handle it as long as you keep your feet covered up. How about we give it a shot together?"

Every alarm bell in my head started ringing. "Oh, I don't want you to do that," I said nervously. "I mean, it's actually getting worse, and the smell… the smell can kill."

This was a complete lie—the fungus was completely gone at this point—but I wasn't about to let her drag me back into the curse.

"Hmm," she said, looking out the window of the cab. After a moment, she turned back to me with that wistful expression she was so good at. "Jake, we could have had such a good time together."

A good time together? I thought. *I'd be dead by now if we were together.*

I was holding Beth's phone number in my hand, the paper soft from my nervous fidgeting. I thought about her laugh, her genuine smile, the way she'd hugged that ridiculous stuffed trout like it was the best gift she'd ever received.

"Yes," I said, looking out my own window and smiling at the thought of calling Beth as soon as I got to Paris. "Isn't it a shame?"

THE END

www.ingramcontent.com/pod-product-compliance
Lightning Source LLC
Chambersburg PA
CBHW050333110726
47899CB00007B/2478

* 9 7 9 8 9 9 9 7 1 9 2 1 8 *